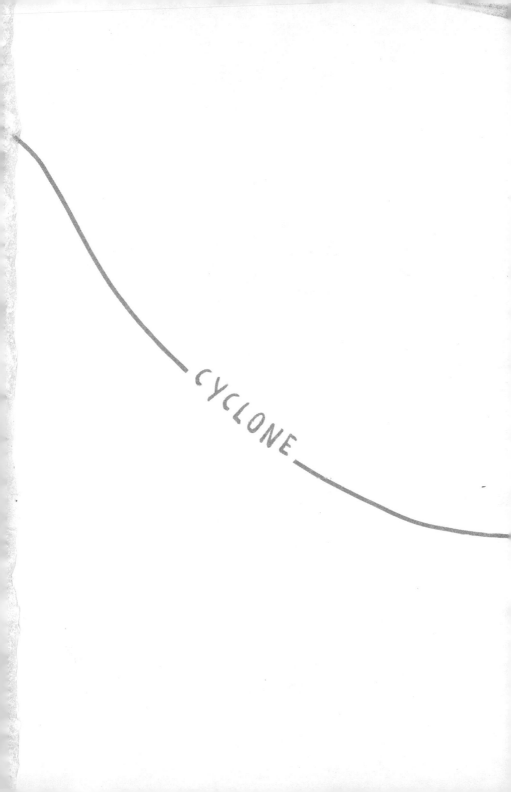

CYCLONE

A CAITLYN DLOUHY BOOK

atheneum Atheneum Books for Young Readers

NEW YORK LONDON TORONTO SYDNEY NEW DELHI

CYCLONE

By
Doreen
Cronin

A atheneum

ATHENEUM BOOKS
FOR YOUNG READERS
An imprint of Simon &
Schuster Children's Publishing
Division 1230 Avenue of the
Americas, New York, New York 10020
ATHENEUM BOOKS FOR YOUNG READERS
is a registered trademark of Simon & Schuster, Inc. Atheneum logo is
a trademark of Simon & Schuster, Inc. For information about special
discounts for bulk purchases, please contact Simon & Schuster Special Sales
at 1-866-506-1949 or business@simonandschuster.com. The Simon &
Schuster Speakers Bureau can bring authors to your live event. For more
information or to book an event, contact the Simon & Schuster Speakers
Bureau at 1-866-248-3049 or visit our website at www.simonspeakers.com.
Book design by Debra Sfetsios-Conover and Brad Mead The text for this
book was set in Melior LT Std. The illustrations for this book were rendered
with an iPad and in pencil. Manufactured in the United States of America
0417 FFG First Edition 10 9 8 7 6 5 4 3 2 1 CIP data for this book
is available from the Library of Congress. ISBN 978-1-4814-3525-3
ISBN 978-1-4814-3527-7 (eBook)

For Samantha Rahni Gottesman

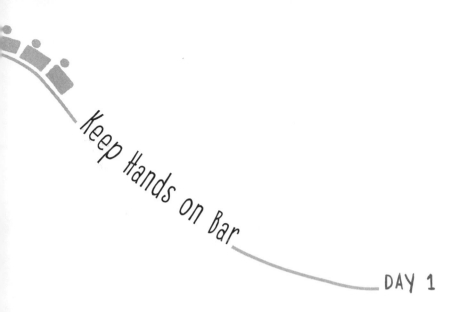

Keep Hands on Bar

The last word I understood completely from my cousin Riley's mouth was the F-bomb. Riley dropped the F-bomb thirty-seven times while we rode the Cyclone roller coaster in Coney Island, Brooklyn. The Cyclone is very, very old.[1] It is made out of wood. It sways. That's right. SWAYS—as in back and forth—just in case plummeting down a six-story drop at high speed wasn't enough for you. I'm making it sound like this didn't worry me— oh, it did. Just not enough to keep me off it. I had

---

[1] Calvin Coolidge was president when the Cyclone was built. It was 1927. TWENTY-SEVEN! And Calvin Coolidge sounds like a made-up name. But it isn't. While we are at it, Ulysses (YOU-LIS-EES) also sounds like a made-up name. Isn't. And honestly, to me, Barack Obama sounded a little made up, but only because it was new to me.

waited a long time to be tall enough (fifty-four inches!) to get on that roller coaster. So I was determined, despite being a little afraid, to take my finally four-and-a-half-foot twelve-year-old self on the oldest wooden roller coaster in the world.

The truth is, I was more than a little afraid of going on the Cyclone. As much as I desperately wanted to ride it—it's *famous*, after all—I very desperately did not want to ride it *alone*. My parents wouldn't go. Heights make my dad turn green, and Mom is not a roller-coaster kind of person. Aunt Maureen—Aunt Mo for short—was out of the question. She gets dizzy on the *merry-go-round*, so that left my cousin Riley, and she is not a big fan of roller coasters either. But she was going on that thing with me—because I was determined. The Cyclone was *the* reason I bugged my dad to bring us to Brooklyn during our yearly trip to Long Island to visit my cousin and aunt. I had even prewritten most of my summer essay on it![2] The assignment was almost done, too. I just needed the part where I actually *rode* the roller coaster. I was now absolutely,

[2] Footnotes and all; with the lackluster title of "The Reeves Family Summer Vacation."

positively *ready for the Cyclone!* At least I thought I was until I was standing in its shadow looking up at it. It looks much smaller on the Internet.

"It's all yours." My dad slapped two Cyclone tickets into my hand with a shake of his head, and I slapped one of them right into Riley's. Riley barely acknowledged me, staring as the roller-coaster cars climbed slowly up to the top of the first drop. *Click-click-click-click.* Riley was already having some serious doubts and insisted that we watch it a few more times. Metal gates and high fencing surrounded its base, making it seem like a dangerous, caged animal. Riley was sure gaping at it like it was. I wished the people riding it weren't screaming so loud; that wasn't helping either.

"Mom," Riley finally said, "*you* should go with Nora. You said you loved roller coasters!"

"Twenty years ago," Aunt Maureen clarified, taking a step backward, away from the ride. "Not now."

"We'll meet you back here in half an hour," said my mother. "For the record, I think you're both crazy." At that, she and my dad and aunt turned and headed toward Nathan's Famous, leaving us gazing up at the monster ride. It took up an entire block.

It even had its own address: 1000 Surf Avenue, Brooklyn.

"Let's get a hot dog too!" said Riley, apropos of nothing, pulling me in the direction our parents had just gone. "I love hot dogs!"

"You do *not* love hot dogs." I swung her back toward the roller coaster. "You *tolerate* hot dogs." It was true. She felt the same way about hot dogs as I do about scrambled eggs—I'll eat them as a last resort, but that's it.

"But these are famous hot dogs!" she practically sang. It was a desperate—and lame—argument, and she knew it.

"Trust me on this, Riley," I said. "The time to eat a hot dog is not right before you get on a roller coaster." The clicking stopped, and we looked up again.

Riley pointed to the four flags whipping around in the wind at the top of the roller coaster—right above where the roller-coaster cars somehow seemed suspended for a second. "What does it say there?"

"I can't see from here," I flat-out lied. LAST WARN-ING. REMAIN SEATED. Riley gasped as a train of coaster cars was suddenly let loose and roared toward the ground. The screams picked up a notch, too.

"How high up is that?" Riley asked.

"I'm not sure." Second lie.[3] The coaster shot around a tight curve at the bottom of the drop and headed up again.

"Oh my God, how fast is that thing going?"

"Pretty fast." Vague lie.[4]

Riley jabbed a finger at me. "I am in charge of the seat belt. We are going to pull it so tight that it cuts off our circulation. Do you hear me?"

"As tight as you want." Lie of omission.[5]

"This is going to be the scariest three minutes of my life!"

"It will be over in less than two!" At last, a truth.[6]

"It better be," she said. We took a few steps toward the Cyclone line, but then she stopped short. "You know what? I'm really hot. Let's go swimming first." She grabbed my arm again and tried to pull me toward the beach. "We'll go swimming and then we can dry off on the roller coaster."

"No." I pulled her back toward the line, a little

---

[3] Eighty-five feet.
[4] Sixty mph.
[5] No seat belts, just a lap bar.
[6] One minute and fifty-five seconds, to be exact.

too hard. "We only have about twenty-five minutes left before Dad comes back. And you know he'll say, 'It's time to go, I don't want to sit in traffic, we have to leave,'" I said in my best dad voice, "and then I'm pretty sure he'll never come back to Brooklyn again and then I'll never get a chance to go on the Cyclone. *Today* is the day." Dad had very little car patience. He had already threatened to turn back around this morning when it took twenty minutes to find a parking spot. The spot we finally found was so far away he wasn't even sure if we were still in Brooklyn.

"Come on, Riley!" I was begging now. I was not above begging. "It will be awesome!"

Riley eyed the cars bolting around a curve in the track. "It's not going to be awesome when I throw up all over you!"

"Listen to me. Remember how you didn't want to boogie board when we went to Bethany Beach two summers ago because the waves were too big?"

"Yeah." Her eyes went wide. The coaster was barreling down a plunge.

"Well, you loved it, right?" I stepped into her line of vision so she had to look at me.

"Yeah, but this is different."

"No, it isn't."

The key to keeping Riley calm was to keep her talking. If she was talking, she was good.

"What if I really do throw up?" Riley asked. She was now twirling a handful of her hair into a long rope. A thick, black, kinked-up-because-her-hair-is-so-curly rope. It actually looked like something I might be able to hold on to. Not a good thought, for either of us.

"You won't. And stop torturing your hair," I said. "Besides, even if you do, it won't gross me out, I promise!" I vomited once after a long run. My heart was racing and it was crazy hot out, and, honestly, I wasn't feeling very well that morning, but I wanted to run. So, yep, right there at the end—*plehhh!* I was mortified at the time, of course, but apparently, I wasn't the first person to puke after a long run on a hot day. I'm pretty sure Riley wouldn't be the first person to puke after a roller-coaster ride either. I eyeballed the current load of passengers, looking for potential pukers. Oh God, don't let Riley see anybody puke when they get off this thing. . . .

"You're gross, Nora!" But she did let go of her hair. "Fine. Fine already. But you owe me a hot dog! If I throw up, you owe me two!"

"Deal!" I whooped. I did not point out the painfully obvious—that eating *two* hot dogs after vomiting was a lousy idea—because I didn't want her thinking any more about the possibility. Riley *was* afraid; she might *actually* throw up. But Riley, being who she is, knew I really wanted to go, knew she was my only hope, and didn't want to disappoint me on my first—and likely last—visit to Coney Island, Brooklyn. That's the kind of cousin she is.

"Okay, let's get this over with already!" *All right!* I knew she would come through!

The line to get on the Cyclone was designed like a switchback trail, zigzagging back and forth to get to the front, and lucky for me, it wasn't very long— less time for Riley to lose her nerve and change her mind. I have to admit my legs already felt a little shaky—my stomach, too. Riley trailed a few steps behind me, so I waited for her to catch up. We stepped aside to let a group of kids—who had all clearly reached the fifty-four-inch mark younger than I had—screaming, "First car! First car!" dash past us. I didn't even want the first car, so I was happy to let them pass. We changed direction at the end of the row. Riley stopped to wave to her mother, who had changed her mind and stayed behind. She waved back—our official send-off. I tried to pick up the pace, but the closer we got, the slower Riley walked. I grasped her hand to urge her along.

"I'm nauseous already," she said with a laugh, but she was squeezing my hand really tightly. And I was glad, partly because I could keep her from bolting and partly because my own stomach was getting progressively questionable. Riley didn't look so hot either. But I kept right on moving, up, up, up—ten more feet, through the turnstile, and we'd be *on* the loading platform!—so when Riley stopped short again, I almost fell backward. Riley wasn't looking at the platform—she was looking at the first hill that loomed over us, five stories high. And she didn't look the laughing kind of scared anymore; she looked *really* scared. She let go of my hand.

"I'm not doing it," she said. Screams pierced the air as the cars plummeted down the first hill. "Nope. I'm done." And she turned around to leave.

"Chicken!" the kids standing behind us teased.

"Riley—c'mon, we're almost there! You can do this, I know you can." I grasped her hand again, and somehow, the line shifted forward and she let me pull her through the turnstile onto the front of the loading platform. The next round of cars would be ours. Riley looked like she was going to cry.

"Riley, you can do this," I said, using my calmest voice, even though my internal voice was shrieking, *Oh my God, we're nearly there, just do it!* The cars pulled into the loading area. Some of the riders were laughing and others were yelling and cursing. One lady's face was drenched with sweat; she still had her eyes closed. The bars lifted and the cars started to empty. "See?" I waved my hand toward the outgoing riders. No pukers! "Everybody survived!"

The guy who was the roller-coaster loader was tall and cute—exactly the distraction I needed. "C'mon, gorgeous," he crooned, winking at Riley. "It's fun. Trust me." Then he barked at the closed-eye lady and two last kids to get off.

"Man, that was awesome!" the kids exclaimed, dropping a few happy F-bombs themselves, high-fiving each other as they climbed out of the car.

"Let's get back in line!" I raised my eyebrows at Riley, in a *see, it's awesome* way. Riley, however, was now looking over their heads at a sign to our left that read: WARNING: THE CYCLONE ROLLER COASTER IS A HIGH-IMPACT RIDE. ANY PERSON WITH BACK, NECK, OR HEART PROBLEMS SHOULD NOT RIDE THIS RIDE. NO PREGNANT PERSON SHOULD RIDE. HOLD ON WITH BOTH HANDS. It might as well have said THIS IS REALLY FAST AND DANGEROUS AND YOU WILL ABSOLUTELY THROW UP. TURN BACK! LAST CHANCE! DON'T DO IT!

But Cute Roller-Coaster Loading Boy came to the rescue once again. My mother says Riley is "boy crazy," but she got attention whether she was looking for it or not. She was curvy with that wild, dark hair and cocoa-brown eyes and, almost always, except for right now, a megawatt smile. Loading Boy smiled at Riley and held out his hand to help her into our car—the third one from the front. Psych! There was no way she was going to chicken out in front of him. Riley took his hand and climbed. Loading Boy did not keep his hand out for me. Riley looked offended on my behalf, but I wasn't there for cute Brooklyn boys; I was there for the roller coaster. "Scooch over!" I said. She slid to the far side. We were in!! And Riley couldn't get out. Success!!

The cars around us filled quickly, with lots of giggles and excited screams. The bar came down and Riley gave it a good, hard shake to make sure it was locked. Loading Boy did the same. I guess Riley forgot about the seat belt. Then she made the sign of the cross, just like Aunt Maureen always did whenever she saw something terrible on the news or found out that somebody died. I was not sure what her mother would think of this casual use of the gesture.

"Ready?" I asked, grinning at my cousin. The car lurched forward and began to slowly rise up the tracks. *Click-click-click.* My heart began to race. We *click-click-click*ed past another sign: KEEP HANDS ON BAR. THIS MEANS DO NOT PUT HANDS UP.

Riley dropped her first F-bomb. To be fair, she wasn't the only one. *Click-click-click.* A chorus of profanity rose up around us. The car rose higher. A tingling feeling traveled up my legs and exploded in my stomach. I made the sign of the cross with one jittery hand, the other tightly wrapped around the safety bar.

F-bomb, F-bomb, F-bomb from Riley as we rolled slowly up the first incline. Another sign. FINAL WARNING. REMAIN SEATED. The car rose higher. The flags we had seen from the ground whipped and waved wildly above our heads. Another heavy *click* sound and we were suddenly suspended at a steep, terrifying angle, gravity practically plastering me to the seat, reminding me how much my body preferred solid ground. Slowly we rose again, our car finally teetering at the top, and then we plunged. *Plunged.* My hair went wild, my face flattened by the pressure and speed of the drop. On the first sharp turn, Riley's body weight shifted, smashing me against the metal wall of the car, adding to the violent sensations of shaking and rattling that were already flooding my body.

"AAAAAAAAHHHHHH!!!!!" I screamed without choice. And I couldn't *stop* screaming. Not for one minute, fifty seconds. I was doing it! I was riding the Cyclone! I was riding the oldest, shakiest roller coaster in the world! And just like that, the cars slowed as we approached the loading platform—it was done.

The bar flipped up. Cute Roller-Coaster Loading Boy helped Riley out of the car, and I, thank you very much, got myself out. I held on to Riley as soon as her feet hit the platform to steady myself. We went down the ramp hand in hand and only let go of each other just long enough to pass through the bright red revolving-door exit gate. The crowd of nonriders, mostly parents—mine, Riley's, the other kids'—were walking toward us, all grinning from ear to ear. My legs were still wobbly, my adrenaline still pumping, I was light-headed—and even a little nauseous. It felt just like crossing the finish line of the Bull Run Invitational cross-country meet (minus the vomit!). Riley held up her phone to take our selfie with the Cyclone behind us. We were arm in arm again and all smiles.

Awesome, right? Except it wasn't.

Because after we got off the Cyclone—after all the researching, writing, footnoting, begging, whining, Loading Boy smiles, sign-of-the-cross-ing, body smashing, and F-bombing, and immediately after the flash went off on her pink phone—my thirteen-year-old cousin, Riley, slipped through my arm and collapsed at my feet.

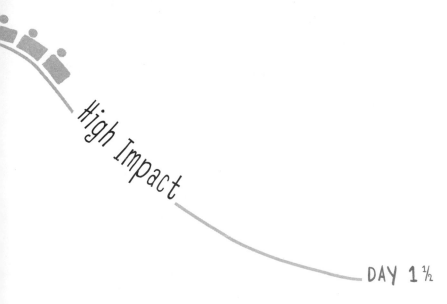

DAY 1 ½

Riley!!"

Our parents ran toward Riley. Strangers ran toward Riley. Everyone moved toward her, except me. I backed *away* from her. I backed away from Riley, and I stared at her lying on the ground.

"Call an ambulance!!" a loud voice bellowed. I picked Riley's phone up off the ground, and I'd like to tell you that I dialed the fastest 911 in the history of 911, but I did not.

I *didn't* call an ambulance.

I *didn't* get down on the ground with her.

I *didn't* grab her by the hand and ask her if she was okay. I just stood there. My limbs went stiff. I held my breath, just waiting for her to get back up.

15

Waiting. Waiting too long. I was the last person to realize that that wasn't going to happen.

"Riley. Riley. Riley. Honey. C'mon, sweetheart. C'mon. Riley. Riley. Riley." Aunt Mo, my mom, and Dad were all on their knees, all pleading with her at the same time.

A man with a little boy at his side pushed his way through the crowd. "GET BACK! I'm a firefighter. Get back! Give her some space!" He crouched beside Riley and, without missing a beat, took a cue from the parents' pleading and jumped in. The firefighter grasped my cousin's wrist, feeling for a pulse. "Riley. Riley. Can you hear me?" He crouched lower and put his ear right to her mouth, suddenly holding her by the jaw and looking inside. "Call an ambulance." He said it calm, but loud.

"I already have," my mom told him quickly. How and when did my mom do that? "What's wrong? Is she okay?"

"What happened here? Did you see anything?" asked Firefighter Dad, ignoring Mom's question. "Did she hit her head? Was she choking?"

"No, no," my mom answered. "She got off the roller coaster, took a few steps, and then . . . she just . . . fainted . . . or something." Aunt Maureen was still clutching Riley's other hand, calling her name over and over. Riley didn't move. Didn't flinch, or twitch, or blink. She just lay there, perfectly still, as still as I've ever seen her.

The only inexplicable impulse I had was to somehow get her beautiful hair off the filthy, sticky concrete. Needless to say, I didn't act on it. I couldn't look at her. I couldn't *not* look at her. And I couldn't move. A little boy with spiky brown hair and a cotton-candy-blue mouth, the firefighter's son, hovered close to his father. His scrubby shoes were almost touching Riley's hair. I wanted him to move his feet. Firefighter Dad was saying something to Riley, leaning so close to her face that I thought she might be telling him something back: *I'm okay, I'm fine. Help me up.* But she wasn't. Aunt Maureen was crying now, holding Riley's hand and calling her name, louder and louder, becoming unhinged. Firefighter Dad's kid started to cry too. I finally did something useful; I reached out to hold the boy's sticky blue hand. I led him back a step or two, mostly to move his dirty shoes away from Riley's hair. That's *all* I did.

The shriek of a siren pierced through the commotion. Paramedics pushed their way through the crowd, rolling a stretcher between them, ordering people to stand back. Everyone obeyed. Firefighter Dad gave them a steady stream of information in a language that was clearly English, but I understood none of it. They strapped Riley to a board, then picked it up and put her on the stretcher. One of the paramedics put an oxygen mask on her face, and the other held it while they wheeled her away. It was fast. It was seamless, almost graceful. It may have taken less time than the roller-coaster ride. Then Aunt Maureen was climbing into the back of the ambulance with Riley, sirens were wailing, lights flashing, and then the ambulance was gone as quickly as it had come. It was a blur. It still is. She was here and then she was not here.

"Nora!" my mother suddenly screamed. I jumped. Why was she yelling at *me*? I think she had forgotten I was even there. I didn't blame her; I didn't feel like I was anywhere until she grabbed me and wrapped her arms around me. The little boy was still attached—or stuck—to my hand.

"They'll take her to the nearest hospital," Firefighter Dad explained to us. In my blur, I thought he had gone with Riley. But, of course not. "It's not far from here. You have a car?" The kid ditched me and ran to his dad. I wiped my hand on my shorts.

"Yes, somewhere . . . ," answered my father, looking around. "It's not very close. I think it's up . . . that way somewhere?" He motioned vaguely.

"We're not from around here," explained my mother. "We're from Maryland. We are just . . . a little turned around here . . . um, I think the car is down that way. . . ."

"Worry about the car later," interrupted Firefighter Dad. He swooped his kid up on his shoulders. "You need to get to the hospital now."

"Here, I can call you a cab," offered a stranger. She was already on her cell phone, her own sweaty, wide-eyed kids in tow. She had been in the crowd too. Across from me. Close to Riley. She had made the sign of the cross as she watched Aunt Maureen cry and plead for Riley to get up. I watched her on the phone—the roller coaster still roared and screeched and screamed. Firefighter Dad was explaining where the hospital was, my dad nodding at all the directions and repeating them back, pointing and gesturing, to confirm. They shook hands. My mother hugged Firefighter Dad. "She'll be okay, right?"

He wiped sweat off his forehead with the back of his arm. "She's young and she's in good hands." My mother nodded and pretended that he had actually answered the question. He looked right at me. "Thank you for watching Zack."

"No, wait!" Cab lady with the phone was pointing toward the street, where somebody else was about to open the door of a taxi that had just arrived at the curb.

"We need that! It's an emergency!" Firefighter Dad boomed, his arm out as if to clear the way for us. The couple at the taxi door stepped aside, no questions asked. We jumped in.

"The hospital, please, quickly," said my dad. The driver peeled into the traffic. Through the window, Zack waved at me and then grabbed a chunk of his dad's hair with his sticky, blue-sugar hands. They merged back into the crowd and disappeared.

"Maybe she just fainted," I offered. As if only we had thrown a glass of water in Riley's face, she would have bounced right back up and asked for a hot dog. Although I'm pretty sure Firefighter Dad would have thrown cold water on Riley's face if he thought that was what she needed.

"You might be right. It is very hot today," added my mom hopefully. "And there is absolutely no shade there. They should have more shade."

"I'm not so sure about that, honey," said Dad. He sounded less hopeful. "Did Riley say anything unusual to you before you got on the roller coaster?"

"Like what?" I snapped. My heart jumped from my chest to my throat.

"I don't know, like she wasn't feeling well, or had a headache, or felt tired? Anything like that?"

You mean, besides *Please don't make me do this*? You mean, besides *I'm scared half to death*? *I'm going to throw up*? *Let's do anything else in the world besides get on this old, wooden, shaky Abraham Lincoln roller coaster*?

"Nope." Lies were just pouring out of me that

21

day. "Nothing like that. She was a little nervous, that's all." Partial lie. She had said she was nauseous but that was from fear—not illness—like what Dad asked about.

"She'll be okay," Mom assured us. "She's probably coming down with a virus or something and the heat made it worse. I bet she's dehydrated. We'll take her home, put her to bed, and fill her up with liquids." She stopped for a second. "If we ever find her. Where the hell is this hospital?" The last word cracked as it came out of her mouth. Traffic was slowing down. "How much farther?" she demanded of the taxi driver.

"Just a few blocks. White building. Up there," the driver answered. We were stopped at another red light.

"Great. We'll get out here." Dad was already pulling money out of his pocket. He handed a twenty to the driver, told him to keep the change even though the fare was only eleven dollars, and then opened the door, pulling me out of the cab. Mom was the last one out, but as soon as we hit the sidewalk, she started to run. I've never seen my mother run before. She actually *sprinted*, dodging traffic as she ignored the DON'T WALK sign. I tried to do the same, but Dad yanked me back on the sidewalk to wait for the light. "Everything is going to be okay, kitten." But my mother running ahead of us as fast as she could felt much more like the truth.

Remain Seated

hat is taking so long?" Aunt Maureen stalked toward the double doors that separated the waiting room from the actual emergency room and then stalked back. After the rush of the sirens, the cab, the running, and the traffic, the sitting in the waiting room was torture. Aunt Mo was growing paler by the minute as she exchanged tense whispers with my mom.

Then Riley's phone rang in my shorts, and I jumped a mile. I had forgotten it was even in there. I pulled it out, and Riley's friend Rachel's face lit up the screen. Hitting decline with my thumb, I put it away at the exact moment my mom gestured for me to turn the ringer off. I stared at the crack running top

24

to bottom on the glass. The sight of it sent another wave of guilt coursing through me. We'd made that crack last night, me and Riley. And Riley had been so mad. She told her mom that we had just been goofing around, which is about as far from the truth as you could get. It had been our biggest fight—our only real fight—ever. The phone suddenly buzzed and I nearly dropped it—Rachel retrying. I hit ignore one more time. But Mom and Aunt Maureen were back in a whisper huddle, so I kept the phone out and scrolled through Riley's texts. I didn't recognize most of the names, although one jumped out at me from the cracked screen.

 GEORGINA: WHERE DID U GO?

 GEORGINA: TEXT ME WHEN YOU CAN.

 GEORGINA: MISS YOU.

They were from last night. Riley had seen them— they were no longer lit up—but she hadn't answered them. Was it because of our fight? Was she keeping her promise to me even though *I* hadn't kept mine?

The low battery warning came up on the screen,

and I decided I'd better save the phone in case of an emergency. Well, in case of *another* emergency. I double-checked that the ringer was off and shoved the phone back in my pocket.

"You okay, kitten?" asked my dad. He was holding a newspaper—but he wasn't reading it, just rolling and unrolling it. Dad is usually really pale and always mostly bald. Which is why he hates the beach. But today his face was bright red with sunburn, which is just one more reason why we shouldn't have gone to Coney Island. But I had begged, a lot. *I've never been to Brooklyn! Coney Island is famous! I need it for my essay! Please!* Worse? Riley hadn't cared where we went. If she had gotten *her* way, instead of me getting mine, we'd be sitting under an umbrella at the beach eating hot dogs right now. Riley would be pointing out who she thought was cute, and I would be pretending to think they were cute too, even though I usually didn't. Let's just say Riley has very *questionable* and—as I discovered last night—dangerous taste in "cute." Ugh. Instead here we were sitting silently, pacing silently, in the middle of an emergency room.

"Mrs. McMorrow?" A woman doctor who

looked much younger than my parents appeared in front of us in blue scrubs.

Aunt Maureen stopped pacing and hurried over. "How is she? Where is she? Is she okay?" she asked as my parents shot up out of their seats.

"Mrs. McMorrow, I'm Dr. Mejia. I'm a pediatric neurologist.[7] I'm afraid I have some serious news." She paused. My aunt went even paler, if that could be possible. "I'm afraid your daughter has had a stroke," Dr. Mejia said quietly. A *what*? Aunt Maureen looked like someone had just punched her in the stomach. Even my dad, who is pretty calm and collected, looked like he might fall over. I wasn't sure I even really knew what a stroke was, but everybody else seemed to know exactly what it meant, and that it was *bad*.

"That's impossible," Aunt Maureen cried out as my mother moved to her side. "She's only thirteen years old! Thirteen-year-olds don't have strokes." Her voice was cracking. Dr. Mejia gestured toward the chairs, and Mom guided Aunt Maureen into

[7] "Pediatric" means dealing with infants, children, and adolescents. Generally birth to eighteen years old (and probably the kind of doctor you see now). A neurologist is a doctor who specializes in the nervous system, which includes your brain, spine, and, well, nerves.

one. I went frozen again. Stiff again. What was wrong with me?

"That doesn't make any sense," my mother stammered at the doctor. "Are you sure it's not something else? It must be something else. . . ." She looked at my dad like he might be able to give her a better answer. My dad lowered his eyes and let out a long, slow breath.

"I'm sorry," said Dr. Mejia. "We're positive, Mrs. McMorrow. Riley has definitely had a stroke. A CT scan[8] confirmed a clot in her brain. It's called an ischemic stroke." Dr. Mejia looked down at some papers in her hand. "But there are some other concerns." Aunt Mo didn't wipe the tears that were spilling over. My mom dug a tissue out of her bag, but Aunt Maureen waved it away.

"Your daughter has a heart condition." ANY PERSON WITH BACK, NECK, OR HEART PROBLEMS SHOULD NOT RIDE THIS RIDE flashed in front of me.

"What kind of heart condition?" said Aunt Maureen, her voice so small. She was looking up at Dr. Mejia now.

---

[8] CT scan is short for CAT scan, which is short for computerized axial tomography, which is a way of taking a picture (scan) inside of your body.

"She has atrial fibrillation,"[9] answered the doctor. "When your daughter came in, her heart was beating too fast.[10] It's likely that a clot in her heart came loose and traveled to her brain."

Aunt Mo didn't even *try* to say anything to that. My mother used the tissue to wipe her own eyes. This wasn't even one terrible thing. It was two terrible things—*stroke* and a *heart problem.* Dr. Mejia sat down next to my aunt. "I know this is an awful lot to take in." It felt like our turn to talk, for someone to say *something*, but Mom, Dad, and Aunt Maureen now all looked how I felt: frozen. I couldn't take it.

"Is she going to be okay?" I asked. Firefighter Dad wouldn't answer the question, but maybe the doctor would.

"We're keeping a very close eye on her," answered Dr. Mejia. We were almost eye level now

[9] The doctor slang for this is "AFib." They only call it atrial fibrillation once. You are expected to catch on pretty quickly and then refer to it as AFib. Which is exactly how I will be referring to it from here on in. It means your heart is quivering more than pumping. Kind of a short circuit in your heart's electrical system. It also means blood isn't pumping through and out of your heart like it should. So it can bunch up and form a clot.

[10] Her heart rate (and yours, too) should be anywhere between sixty and one hundred, depending on age, height, weight, etc. Fifty-five to eighty-five is about average, though.

that she was sitting. "Are you Riley's sister?"

"No, her cousin," I answered, more to the floor than to her face. That one question was all I had, and nobody would answer it.

Dr. Mejia smiled and turned back to Aunt Maureen, putting a hand on her arm. "I'm afraid we won't know the full extent of the damage for another twenty-four to forty-eight hours or so. You can see her now, but only for a few minutes. She's conscious, but we are concerned about paralysis on the right side of her body. In strokes affecting this part of the brain, it is also common for the patient to have issues with speech and swallowing.[11] We're hoping both will be temporary." Dr. Mejia was both kind and matter-of-fact at the same time. She didn't feel like part of an emergency.

Aunt Maureen attempted to stand up, but a loud sob bent her in half. My mom pulled her close and stroked her hair, like she was a child.

"Take your time," said the doctor. "It's okay. Take your time. I'll walk you back when you're

[11] The brain has quite a few different parts. I have drawn a picture for you at the end of the book, because otherwise my footnote would be very long and possibly confusing.

30

ready." *Ready?* How could you be ready for this?

Aunt Maureen buried her face in my mother's neck, her shoulders shaking as she cried. I didn't want to cry, but it was impossible not to. My throat tightened and I pressed my lips together. The lump in my throat was too big to hold. Aunt Maureen finally wiped her eyes and stood up straight. "Please, let's go. Riley needs me." Her regular voice was back. Mom and Aunt Mo followed Dr. Mejia through the NO ADMITTANCE double doors and out of the waiting room.

"Should we go too?" I asked my dad.

"Not right now," he said. "Let her mom see her first."

So this is awful to say, but I was relieved. Awful, I know, but I was afraid to see Riley. She couldn't talk and her body was paralyzed, which even I knew meant she couldn't move, and she had a *stroke* and a *heart problem*, and what would that look like?

I watched another doctor come out and talk to an elderly woman who was sitting by herself. I couldn't hear what the doctor was saying, but she didn't smile and she didn't sit down next to the lady. What was her emergency? I wondered.

The room was practically full. How many different emergencies could there be?

"Dad? What's a stroke, exactly?"

"It's when a blood vessel in your brain gets blocked or bleeds," he explained. He hugged me close and kissed the top of my head. I could feel his hot sunburn on my face.

"So . . . why wouldn't she be able to talk?" I asked.

"Well, when you have a stroke, part of your brain doesn't get the oxygen it needs . . . and then it's damaged," he answered. I don't know why he knew so much about having a stroke, because I'd never once heard him even say the word.

"Is she going to be okay?" I had to ask again.

"I don't think we know yet, kitten." I ran my thumb over the edge of Riley's phone in my pocket. It felt a little greasy, probably from my own sweat. I ran my finger along the crack.

Dad shook some change around in his hand and sorted through the coins. "We just have to wait and see." He held out a bunch of quarters and dimes. "Why don't you grab us a water from the vending machine?"

I had one more question, even though I had a horrible feeling about the answer. In fact, I *knew* the answer. Question: "How does a blood clot move from your heart to your brain?" Answer: WARNING: THE CYCLONE ROLLER COASTER IS A HIGH-IMPACT RIDE. ANY PERSON WITH BACK, NECK, OR HEART PROBLEMS SHOULD NOT RIDE THIS RIDE. So I didn't even ask Dad. I took the money instead and headed for the vending machine. When I looked back at my dad, I noticed that he looked scared. I had never once seen my dad look scared before. It was a strange face for him, and he looked like a very different father from the one I was used to. He laid tho nowspapor on the empty seat beside his; it wasn't enough to distract him anymore. A man a few seats down gestured toward the newspaper. "Finished?"

"All yours," said Dad, with his new face that was also missing his usual smile.

My pocket was vibrating again. I took the phone out and shoved it back in my pocket without looking.

Critical

S he's still the same," my mother announced as she came back through the emergency-room doors without Aunt Maureen. Dad and I both jumped up as soon as we saw her. And there was no real news. "She's in critical condition,[12] and they are working to stabilize her."

"Should we call Elayne?" my dad asked my mom. My aunt Elayne is my mom's other sister. She lives in San Francisco. I hadn't seen her in years.

"It's not like she's going to fly out here, Mike."

"She might, Paige," my dad said gently. "She

---

[12] Critical condition is terrible. The only worse condition is, well, dead. It is the worst of the "conditions" you can be in. The *others* are good, fair, and serious, and I think they are self-explanatory.

might not have much of a choice." My parents exchanged tense glances. "Do you want me to do it?"

"No, I'll do it," she answered, wiping her nose with the back of her hand.

"What about . . . Pete?" Dad asked this even more hesitantly. I couldn't remember the last time somebody brought up Uncle Pete. He and Aunt Mo divorced four years ago, so Uncle Pete is now Former Uncle Pete. He was part of our family—and then he was not. Even Riley rarely mentions him.

"I'm sure he's the *last* thing on Maureen's mind," Mom said tersely, her face a twist.

"He *is* Riley's father; he should know." Dad said this carefully, like he was talking to someone who was about to explode. Normally, this was not a conversation they would have in front of me. But emergencies changed all the rules, I was learning. "I can't imagine"—my dad started, his own voice cracking—"what if . . . ?" He looked at me oddly for a split second and then turned away.

"That's a decision only Maureen can make," Mom answered sharply, but then she softened. "I don't think he would help the situation. They haven't spoken in two years, and Maureen doesn't even know where he is." Mom slumped down into a chair and sat with her eyes closed. Her face was puffy, and sunburn streaked the front of her legs. "I just can't believe this," she said with a sob she couldn't choke back. Without a word, the man in the chair next to her got up to make way for my father. Dad wrapped his arms around her while she cried. Nobody stared or pointed or shifted uncomfortably. A woman nearby offered me her seat too. I shook my head. There was a hierarchy of emergency seating, too, something else I was learning.

When Mom stopped crying, she disappeared again behind the NO ADMITTANCE doors. She was gone only a few minutes. This time when she came back, even puffier-faced, she stopped outside the door and waved Dad over, out of earshot. After a brief conversation, and a few head shakes, my dad went through the NO ADMITTANCE doors and my mom walked toward me.

"Aunt Mo . . ." My mother stopped and took a big breath. "Mo thinks it would be a good idea for you to see Riley."

"She's better?" I asked. What I was really thinking was, *Who, me? Now?*

"She's . . . the same," Mom answered. "But we're all going to stay here tonight. Just to be close. Dad is going to see her now and then you and I will go . . . together." The last time my mother stayed in a hospital overnight, my grandmother had died. Nobody had said anything about Riley dying! There were only two things I knew to worry about—stroke and heart condition. They were serious things. But *dying*? Had I missed the third thing—she could die?

Dad came back through the swinging double doors now, *his* eyes swollen. He hadn't been gone that long. Why were they rushing? What was the hurry to get me in there? Yet another person stood up, offering a seat. He knew. The stranger knew. He knew the third thing! Dad didn't take the seat. He caught Mom's eye and nodded toward the doors. Mom grasped my hand. Our turn. I forced my legs to move.

The emergency room was actually one huge room divided into small sections by sheets hanging from movable tracks, like shower curtains. Mom parked me outside one of the curtained areas and told me to stay put. In the split second that the curtain was drawn back, I saw all I needed to see. It was worse than Riley lying on the concrete. Worse than Riley on a stretcher and being rolled away into an ambulance. I caught my breath.

It was awful.

Riley was riddled with needles, wires, tape, and tubes. Her skin was grayish-blue, and even her lips were pale. Clear liquid dripped from bags hanging off poles by her bed. Nothing about her said "okay." Nothing about her even said "alive."

What had I done? For the second time that day, I backed away from her. I stared down at the floor, my red sneakers blurry through tears. WARNING: THE CYCLONE ROLLER COASTER IS A HIGH-IMPACT RIDE. ANY PERSON WITH BACK, NECK, OR HEART PROBLEMS SHOULD NOT RIDE THIS RIDE.

"Honey."

I looked up. "Nora—oh, honey . . ." My mom. Hugging me. Hard. Rocking me back and forth. "It's okay. It's okay," she said, squeezing so tight as I began to cry. I didn't hear Aunt Maureen; I felt her arms wrapping around the both of us. Riley's curtain was wide open now. I closed my eyes so hard I saw stars.

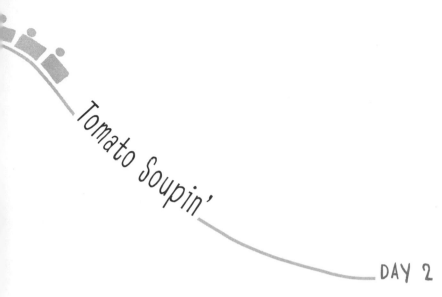

Tomato Soupin'

Archie . . ."

I wiped sleep out of my eyes when I heard the dog's name. When I sat up, the pieces around me fell into place. The waiting room, the double doors, Riley. I put my head back down in my dad's lap. How many hours had gone by? My mother was sitting by my feet, talking about the dog. Why were they talking about the dog?

"He'll be scared and hungry," she continued. "And here's a list of what Maureen needs from the house. She won't be home for a few days, at least." My mother was back in control mode. "Throw some things in a bag for me, too."

"You're not coming home?" I was fully awake

now. "Am I staying too? Is Riley okay?" At some point last night my mother had pulled back her hair and washed her face. Yesterday's smudged mascara was gone.

"You're going to go with Dad."

"I'll go get the car." My dad was counting bills from his wallet. "I'm sure I can get a cab in front of the hospital." I stood up to go with him. "You stay here, kitten. It may take me a while to find it. . . ." He kissed the two of us good-bye.

My mother took a deep breath before she finally answered my question about Riley. "Riley is in intensive care now. She had a rough night and developed some swelling in her brain."[13] She reached out and took my hand before I could react. "The doctors say this isn't unusual after a stroke, and they know how to treat it."

"Does it hurt?" My tears came without sound when I imagined Riley's brain building up pressure.

"I don't think so, sweetheart." Mom pulled me toward her. "Riley is getting all kinds of medicine

[13] The medical term for swelling is "edema," no matter where it happens. You can have edema in the brain or in your ankle.

to make sure that she's comfortable." *Comfortable.* Making someone comfortable did not sound the same as making someone better. It had been less than twenty-four hours and things were getting even worse.

"Are you sure it's okay to leave?" Was that right? Were you supposed to leave people behind at the hospital? Riley's brain is swelling, so Mom and Aunt Maureen have to stay? Riley's brain is swelling, but Dad and I have to go home to walk the dog? Riley had a rough night, but Aunt Mo needs clean clothes? Riley is not better, but Riley is comfortable?

"Come on, I want you to eat something before you head back." Mom pulled a bagel and a chocolate milk out of a bag I hadn't even noticed. I didn't take them from her. "It's okay to go home for a bit, honey. And it's okay to eat. Maybe even take a quick shower when you're there. You'll feel better." She offered the bagel again, but I didn't want it. I had no right to be comfortable.

"You feeling okay, kitten?" It had taken Dad about an hour to find the car and drive back to get me.

41

Mom closed the rear door of the car and sent us off with the breakfast I still hadn't eaten and a promise to text if anything changed.

"Yeah." I stared at the hospital from the backseat and wondered which floor Riley was on.

"You feel like talking?"

"Not really." I let my head fall against the window, making myself as uncomfortable as I could.

"Maybe sleep a little more, if you can." I looked down toward the beach as Dad made a left turn onto the parkway at the same corner where Mom had taken off running less than twenty-four hours ago. Looked like any other intersection. You'd never know there was a stroke and brain swelling on the other side.

As much as I didn't want to think about Riley, the only thing I wanted to think about less was her dog. For Riley's sake, I pretend to love Archie because, well, because she loved him and it was important to her. Truth is, he was an overly anxious dog the size of a small pony, with a deep, relentless bark that made the walls shake. It's not that the barking (or the dog, for that matter) scares me, it doesn't, but it *bothers* me because it sounds so urgent—like a crucial point he's making over and over again that I just can't understand.

When Grandma was alive—which she was up until a few years ago—she lived in the house too. Well, it was actually her house, and Riley and her mom moved there after the divorce. She was not a big fan of the dog either, but he came with Mo and Riley, so she put up with it, with a smile on her face too. Grandma called it "tomato soupin'"[14] because even if you didn't like it, if it came with somebody you loved, you had to eat it.

I was tomato soupin' Riley's dog.

Well, Archie, who admittedly hadn't been out since yesterday morning, must have heard the car pull into the driveway, because he was barking his head off before Dad even had the key in the lock. He was too big and too excited to hold back and charged right past us out the door. My father lunged and managed to grab ahold of his collar. Archie barked his bone-rattling bark, furious. Dad wrestled him back inside and grabbed his leash off

---

[14] I would have called it "pea soupin'" because I like tomato soup just fine. Grandma clearly had issues with it.

the banister. "Sorry, boy, long night," he offered, clipping the leash on as Archie dragged him back out the door. *I* headed straight upstairs toward Riley's room, barely sidestepping a giant pile of dog business in the hallway.

Riley's "room" was the space at the top of the stairs that Grandma had originally used as a "sitting area." It was really just an alcove between the two bedrooms and right smack in the middle of everything, which was exactly where Riley wanted to be. If you came upstairs, you had to see her. But she really was one of those people who it is always good to see. When Grandma died, Riley had a chance to take her room—a real room!—but she turned it down because she loved her open space at the top of the stairs. "But there's no door!" I said. "You have no privacy."

"What do I need privacy for?" asked Riley. Who doesn't want privacy? Riley was the only teenage girl in the world who didn't want privacy. Although she sure had secrets. Well, *one*, I now thought, a flash of anger coming over me. Her phone was still in my pocket. I pulled it out—it was dead. But if I plugged it in, I knew exactly what would pop up:

GEORGINA

I tossed the phone into her desk drawer and slammed it shut.

I looked around her room—I'd actually never spent any real time in it without Riley. It was a total mess. I had an inexplicable urge to put everything away, make the bed. Which was weird, because my room is no neater. But at the same time, I didn't want to touch anything. How could the Riley in this room and the Riley in critical condition in the hospital have only one day between them? How was that possible??? The outfits she had tried on and rejected yesterday morning lay on the floor below the mirror, the towel she'd used to dry her hair in a damp lump on top of them. I left everything there and lay down on the unmade bed. I could smell Riley's coconut shampoo on the pillow. I breathod it in, and then, overwhelmed by the smell, I threw the pillow on the floor with everything else from yesterday morning.

"We're back!" my dad announced from the front door, as if he needed to, with Archie barking his head off and his giant body bounding up the stairs to Riley's room. He sat a few feet from the bed and stared at me, like I was hiding Riley somewhere and playing a game with him. Dissatisfied that I couldn't produce her, he started to bark. Over and over. *Where is she? Where is she? Where is she?*

It was the first time that I had ever understood him.

DAY 2½

Forty-eight hours. That's how long Dr. Mejia had said it was going to take before we would know if things were going to be kind of okay, or not okay at all (or the "third thing," which nobody said out loud). And twenty-four of them were gone. Riley was going to be in the Pediatric Intensive Care Unit for a while.[15] Intensive care is exactly what it sounds like: it's where they keep you when you need somebody looking at you all the time (intensively) to make sure you don't die. When you get to a regular room, it's no guarantee that you won't die—you

---

[15] In hospital lingo, the "Pick You." Babies are treated in the Neonatal Intensive Care Unit—the NICU—pronounced "Nick You." Grown-ups who need extra watching are in the plain old intensive care unit, which, if the rule applied, would be pronounced "Ick You," but the rule is not applied, so it is pronounced "I-C-U" (*I see you*). For obvious reasons, I think.

might still die, but they aren't afraid you are going to do it if they take their eyes off you for more than a minute. Maybe they weren't afraid of Riley *suddenly* dying anymore, but they hadn't ruled it out, either. Each "room" on this hall was more of a glass cube— each with its own sliding glass door into the hallway. The rooms made it very easy to be watched closely, and plenty of people were watching.

Riley had been brought to the hospital quickly enough to get a powerful drug that can help within a few hours after a stroke—and that was good. The swelling in her brain had not gotten any worse—and that was good. But she still had an abnormal heart rate, and that needed to be addressed with different medicines and, Dr. Mejia had warned us, possibly surgery.

The PICU, as serious as it was, was made to look and feel like someplace that wasn't . . . terrible. The walls were bright, and a ribbon of blue river was painted on the floor. The plain green scrubs[16] the

---

[16] The same-color shirt and pants that doctors and nurses sometimes wear. They're called scrubs because they're the clothes surgeons wear when they wash up—or "scrub in"—for surgery. Medical professionals' clothes can get kind of gross—bloody, even—so they can throw away the scrubs if they get really disgusting. I like them because it makes the doctors and nurses easy to spot.

doctors and nurses in the emergency room wore were replaced by purple and pink ones. One nurse wore scrubs covered in bright green smiling frogs. The Crayola colors and happy animal faces made you feel like things were a little better here. Some of the harshness—and frankly, terror—of the ER[17] were gone.

"I'll meet you back here in a little while." Mom deposited Dad and me in the PICU "family room"— another sunshine-bright place with a kitchen, a flat-screen television, and children's drawings covering the walls. Even the chairs were cheerful: big and round and comfy, pink and green and blue, with puffy ottomans. Riley would definitely appreciate the colors in this room. There'd been only one thing Riley had changed about Grandma's sitting room when she'd taken it over: the color. The dark wood of Grandma's built-in bookcases? Now a very Riley shade of bright purple.

"Help yourself, please." An older woman was looking up from her magazine and pointing at an open box of doughnuts on the counter next to the

---

[17] Emergency room.

refrigerator. I guess she could tell we were new. Dad grabbed a jelly doughnut while I wandered over to the fish tank on the other side of the room. The tank was huge, with an underwater garden of green plastic plants and fake pink coral, a scattering of "logs" along the graveled bottom—too huge for the two fish that swam in it. I wasn't sure what kind of fish they were—my fish identification skills were pretty much limited to goldfish—but one was blue, with an enormous fan-shaped tail, and the other was a simple but sturdy-looking yellow one about two inches long. It looked like a beginner fish.

Fish don't live that long, so I now wondered whose job it was to make sure that the PICU families didn't start their day with the sight of a dead fish floating in the tank. Did they replace them with new ones? So no one would notice?

"Mr. Reeves? Nora?" A woman I had never seen before came in and called us by name. My heart skipped a beat. Was there news?

"I'm Monica. I'm a child life specialist here at the hospital." Dad had clearly been expecting her, as he pulled out a chair for her and waved me over to the table. "How are you doing today?" Monica asked, looking first at Dad, then me. But she waited on me to respond.

"Okay," I muttered. Was she here for *me*?

"I know it's been a difficult twenty-four hours." She did? What did she know? "And I hear that you are going to visit Riley today for the first time in intensive care." Monica was making what I can only describe as prolonged eye contact—like she was trying to read me somehow. I kept her gaze as long as I could, but then had to look away. "I just wanted to drop by and talk a little so you know what to expect and to help you understand how important you all are to Riley's recovery. All of you—and all of us here at the hospital—are going to work together as a team."

"Okay." Dad nodded along.

"First off, some easy stuff: visiting hours. We only allow two people at a time in PICU, but parents don't count as visitors, so your aunt Maureen can be with Riley all the time. She even has her own chair that opens up into a bed. I promise, we'll take good care of her, too." So maybe Monica wasn't just here for me.

"That's great," Dad said, nodding and maintaining prolonged eye contact, as required.

"And here, in the family room, we want you to be as comfortable and as rested as you can be, as well. This room is always open, and lots of families bring in snacks or cookies to share. Please help yourself, but we ask that you don't bring those types of things into the patients' rooms. It's hard for patients to watch people eat things that they can't eat . . . just yet."

"Riley can't eat?" Dr. Mejia hadn't said anything about not *eating*.

Monica nodded like I'd asked a very clever question. "Stroke patients can often have a hard time swallowing—and that's unsafe. Right now, Riley is getting all the nutrients she needs through a tube. When she's ready, she may be able to try some soft foods. That'll be a part of her recovery." She paused. "Do you have any questions so far?" I had a million of them, but nothing I could articulate. "There's also a food court downstairs that you may have found already. That's open from six a.m. to midnight every day. At the nurses' station, you'll find a folder with take-out and delivery menus, as well."

"That's a lot of options," joked my dad.

"We like to keep our families well fed," Monica said, smiling, "because you are all so important to Riley's recovery—you are all a part of her team." She went on to explain a few more things about Riley's team: her pediatric neurologist[18] (Dr. Mejia, of course) her pediatric cardiologist,[19] and an incredible staff of ICU nurses who I would see all the time. Now she turned directly toward me.

"So, now let's talk about Riley for a few minutes, and what you can expect when you see her this morning." How bad was this going to be? It dawned on me that Monica was managing my expectations. That's what my running coach would call it, as in the newbie runners shouldn't expect to be the first ones across the finish line. Strive for it, yes. Beat yourself up because you don't accomplish it, no. Vomit when you cross the finish line? Maybe. All this talk about visiting before the visiting was actually making me queasy—and I had an urge to run.

Monica gave me a look as though she could

---

[18] In case you forgot, a brain and nervous system doctor.
[19] Heart doctor.

tell I felt a little queasy! I tried to erase any Little Queasy look from my face. Must have worked, because she continued with "Riley is in her own room. You probably saw when you came off the elevator." Riley would actually love a glass cube for a room. It would be perfect for her. "The very first thing you need to do when you go into the room is to wash your hands. Riley's body doesn't have any extra energy to fight off germs and bacteria now . . . so that's the number one rule. Clean hands. There are wires and tubes and machines in the room. It's okay to touch Riley if your hands are clean, but it's important not to touch the tubes and wires and machines. Okay?"

I nodded, biting around the skin on my nails. I hadn't even considered touching Riley.

"It's very common for stroke patients to lose their speech, just like Riley has. Sometimes it comes back, often very slowly. She may try to talk to you, but the words may not come out right—or at all. That might be confusing and a little scary for you."

Riley couldn't talk. Got it. Dad reached over and gently moved my hand away from my mouth to get me to stop chewing on my fingers.

"As you probably know, Riley has some paralysis, which is also very common after a stroke. One side of her body has been affected, but often, just like speech, as she recovers, she may get the use of her arm and leg back. She also has some facial paralysis on the same side, so she will look a little different."

Riley couldn't walk. Got it. Knew that. One side of her *face* was paralyzed. Did not know that. What did that look like?

"Any questions so far?" Another long pause.

"No," I said quickly, earning me a *you said that too quickly* face from Monica.

"Another thing to try to keep in mind is that things can often change quickly in intensive care." She waited, letting that sink in.

"What do you mean? Change how?" asked Dad, looking caught off guard for the first time in the conversation.

"We say the only thing certain about intensive care is uncertainty. Patients can seem very sick in the morning, only to look and sound more like themselves by lunch, only to seem to slide back a bit the next day. Try to take each moment—good or bad—as it happens." More silence sinking in.

Now Monica pulled out a generic picture of a grown-up in a glass cube room, like the ones in the PICU. "This is not a real patient," she explained, "but these are some of the things you may see." Dad and I got a crash course in some of the equipment in the room and what they monitored—the most basic of which were vital signs, or "vitals," and those were the numbers on her monitor. If you've ever been to the doctor (and I'm hoping you have), you've likely had your vitals taken. One of the numbers is your temperature, one is your heart rate (HR), one is how many breaths you take in a minute (RES), BP is blood pressure (which is the force of the blood pushing through your arteries— think of water in a hose), and one that you may not know is called SpO_2,[20] which, Monica explained to

---

[20] You might think it is pronounced, well, Spoh Two (rhymes with Low Two). [I mean, wouldn't you if, say, you were in class and it was your turn to read out loud and the sentence was "Her SPO_2 was not good."] In hospital-speak, however, it's "Pulse-Ox," which I took upon myself to shorten to P-SOCKS. Seriously, P-SOCKS. Your P-SOCKS right now should be more than 96 percent. Which means your blood is carrying 96 percent of the oxygen it is capable of carrying. A P-SOCKS less than 90 means something is wrong. A P-SOCKS less than 80 and you are heading for big trouble. In my defense, if I had known Riley had AFib and lousy P-SOCKS, I never would have dragged her on that stupid roller coaster in the first place.

us, is how much oxygen is being carried in your blood. It's measured by a clip that goes over the tip of your finger.

Dad wasn't looking at Monica. He was looking at me. Trying to read my face. The more she talked, the more anxious I became. The pink ottomans and the fish tank weren't really helping me anymore. Only when she added that Riley would probably be asleep, or possibly sedated,[21] did some of my panic subside. When Riley was ready, her friends would also be allowed to visit, but nobody knew for sure when that would be. For now, it was just us. Just family. Just *the team.*

"And I think that's probably enough for right now. Do you have any questions? Nora? Mike?" We didn't. "Also, Nora, I know you want to see Riley, but it's important for you to know that you *can* change your mind about visiting her. That's okay too."

"Really?"

Monica seemed quite certain of this, but Dad shot me a look. Monica caught that look. She really

---

[21] Taking mediation that puts you in an even deeper sleep than regular sleep, mostly so your body can rest and heal.

was a child life specialist. Dad stood up and shook her hand and thanked her for her time. So I did the same.

"I'm here for Riley, but I'm really a part of *your* team too," she assured us. "Anything you need, just ask."

Could you repeat the part about choosing whether or not I want to visit Riley? was what I wanted to ask, but I didn't. I smiled, I sauntered over to the doughnuts, then back to my spot in front of the fish tank. I named the yellow one AFib and the blue one P-SOCKS.

"So you had a chat with Monica?" Mom asked as she poured a cup of coffee for herself when she came into the family room kitchen a short while later. She looked completely disheveled.

"Yeah," I answered. "She's nice."

"Was it helpful?"

"I guess so." I did guess so. Or maybe it was too early to tell. My parents had a short conversation out of earshot before Dad and I left to follow the happy blue river to Riley's room.

Monica's generic photo of a stranger in intensive

care did not actually prepare me for the sight of *Riley* in intensive care. I bit at the inside of my cheek as I took in her neck and chest, her wrists, even her face, checkered with tape and tubes. Her cube room looked like the control room of a spaceship—screens, double monitors, machines and computers connected to tubing and wires connected all over Riley's body connected to bags and poles and dripping liquids. Riley's bed was tilted forward, her head raised at an angle, a constant beep announcing her heartbeat. I thought she would be different. I thought I would *see* Riley, *recognize* Riley. I thought even though she couldn't talk and couldn't swallow and couldn't walk, she would *be* Riley now that she was in a room with a real bed and a team. But she wasn't. Despite all my managed expectations, a wave of nausea hit me and I backed away from the open door. Dad stayed right beside me.

But Aunt Maureen was smiling at me and gesturing for us to come in. "Look who's here, honey," she crooned to Not Riley, stirring her. Her sleeping chair was still open and unmade. She didn't look like she had slept for a minute. Before I could even step into the room, she pointed to the sink. "Hands first, thanks, Nora." Right, I had already forgotten that part. *The most important thing,* Monica had said. I beat my dad to the sink and washed my hands as long as I could. Cleanest hands in Brooklyn. Maybe the United States. Then he was next to me, nudging me out of the way.

"Uncle Mike and Nora are here to say hello," Aunt Mo was saying. Arrgh! I thought Riley was going to be asleep! I looked over her head at the numbers blinking on a screen.

"Hi, Riley. How are you doing today?" Dad's voice was low and soft, a hospital kind of voice. Riley turned her head our way in slow motion. Only one of her eyes was completely open, like a broken doll. She didn't say anything, but her machines beeped steadily. *Beep beep beep.* The very last thing she looked was comfortable.

I managed a small wave despite the pit in my stomach. Riley slow-motion turned her head back toward Aunt Mo. Saliva dribbled out of the side of her mouth as she murmured a garbled string of sounds. Aunt Mo gently wiped her face and listened closely, as if the sounds made any sense.

"Good girl! Good work!" she cooed. Riley closed her eye.

"She's so happy to see you both," Aunt Mo said, her own eyes bright despite the dark circles underneath. "She's been awake a bit today and I can see her brain is sparking, can't you?"

"Absolutely," my dad assured her, while I nodded. I didn't see any spark. I didn't see any anything but spit and tubes. Dad pulled a chair in a little closer to the bed and sat down. When I sat down, I slid my chair a little bit farther from the bed.

"Did *you* get any sleep?" Dad asked my aunt.

"Enough," answered Aunt Mo. That was a lie. She looked like she hadn't slept in days. The dark circles made her look ghostly pale. She was the same color as Riley.

"Lots of machines, right, Nora?" she said to me. I found something new to look at—a small black ball hovering in a plastic spigot on the wall. It was plugged into an outlet marked OXYGEN. I instinctively checked her P-SOCKS—ninety-seven. Okay. Ninety-seven was good.

"We spent a little time with Monica," Dad went on before I could answer. "The child life special—"

"Child life specialist!" Aunt Mo finished over him. "Who knew there was such a thing? Riley and I met her earlier this morning. We liked her. Didn't we, Riley?" There was no answer from Riley. I was relieved that Aunt Maureen didn't look like she was waiting for one either. "What did you think, Nora?"

"She was nice," I agreed. *She said I didn't have to be here,* I wanted to add. I didn't. But you knew that.

"It's a good thing . . . that they have that. Child specialist, I mean." Dad was looking at me, like I had some wisdom to impart, being a child and all. "Family room is nice too." I began to understand that small talk was the name of the game here. Not medical talk. Not P-SOCKS, not even, *Is she getting any better?*

"Isn't it, though! That's where your mom has been sleeping," Aunt Maureen told us. "I had to practically drag her down there last night and unfold the bed myself. Some of those chairs open up like this one. It's a nice room."

"They have doughnuts, too," I said. Yep, I talked about doughnuts.

Beep beep beep.

"I saw that," Aunt Maureen enthused. "Maybe tomorrow on your way in you could bring a dozen doughnuts or some bagels. You know there's a good bakery up by the gas station . . . at home. . . . You know the one, Mike?"

"I do. We will. Absolutely." I caught Dad checking his watch while Aunt Mo went back to studying Riley's face. "Should we . . . ?"

Beep beep beep.

"Oh yes," answered Aunt Maureen, glancing away from Riley for the briefest moment. "I think Riley has had enough excitement for now. Don't you think so?" She was looking at Riley, not asking us. This time she looked like she might be waiting for an answer. Did Riley answer sometimes? She tucked some of Riley's dark hair behind one ear. Even Riley's hair seemed limp. "We'll see you guys again later. After some rest." She stood up and Dad leaned across the bed and kissed Aunt Maureen on the cheek.

"We'll be back soon, Maureen."

"And thank *you* for coming, Nora. If you find your mother in the family room, see if you can convince her to take a nap—or at least eat something. She's exhausted."

Beep beep beep.

"I will." I smiled. With that, we were done. That was an intensive care visit.

"How did it go?" Mom was waiting for us outside the room. I wondered if she had been watching us through the glass, to see how we did in there.

"Good," answered Dad. "Good." I nodded in agreement. I was a team player and I had done my job. To sit in a chair and exchange awkward tomato-soup smiles with Aunt Mo. The numbers blinked. Riley beeped. The tiny oxygen ball floated in its own plastic space and its very own outlet. My expectations had been managed and I was excused for the day. Was that good? Sure. Okay.

I spent the next few hours dozing off in front of the fish tank, working on summer math homework, flipping through the channels on the television and giving in to my doughnut urges—all three of them. Dad did mostly the same, minus the homework.

We had planned on another visit with Riley, but she was in and out of her room all day with more tests and more scans to track the swelling in her brain. Mom appeared in the family room at seven thirty with a bag of dirty clothes to take home, since both she and Aunt Mo had finally changed.

"Maybe a quick good-bye to Riley before you head home," she ordered in the form of a suggestion.

Dad and I walked hand in hand back to Riley's room, my stomach knots kicking in about twenty feet from her door. As we got closer, I heard it— my aunt Mo crying. I tugged on Dad's arm and he stopped a few feet from the door. Through the window, we could see Aunt Mo's head on Riley's chest and a hospital blanket draped over her shoulders. I got the feeling my mother had wrapped her sister in it before she left the room. I also got the feeling that Aunt Mo had waited for my mother to leave before she cried.

I stared at Riley's heart rate on the monitor.

Seventy.

Beep, beep, beep.

Sixty-eight.

Beep . . . beep.

Dropping.

Sixty-five.

Beep.

Riley must have just fallen asleep. Aunt Mo hadn't just waited for my mother to leave, she also waited until Riley couldn't see or hear her cry, either.

"Okay," Dad began, "we should . . . maybe . . . um . . . leave them . . . alone. We'll see them first thing in the morning." But Dad didn't move, and I didn't either. From the window, I stared at Riley and listened to her heart slow down.

Beep.

Wait.

Beep.

Wait.

Beep.

The crying stopped. Aunt Mo was asleep now too.

"Good night, Riley," Dad whispered, his voice catching.

In the car, I tossed the bag my mother had given us onto the floor, and the clothes Riley had been wearing on the Cyclone spilled out next to the empty water bottles and food wrappers. I gathered them up quickly and made a neat pile on my lap, the denim shorts first, then her purple bra, and finally her black tank top, carefully smoothing out the wrinkles. I sniffed them, expecting coconut, but they smelled like sweat and deodorant and hospital. I put them back in the bag and let it slide to the floor.

PICU

DAY 3

I had a sneaking suspicion that Monica may
have mentioned something about my visiting
"options," because on the drive to the hospital
the next morning, Dad told me that I would be
"visiting" Riley just once a day. I could do that.
I could do once a day. Mom and Dad would sit
with Riley together while I stayed behind in the
family room.

Dad had been a man with a mission this morning, stopping first at the bakery Aunt Maureen had
mentioned to buy pastries, then at the Dunkin'
Donuts for a hundred Munchkins, and then the
bagel store for a dozen bagels. He would have made
six more stops if Aunt Mo had asked. It took both

of us to carry all the food into the family room.

"Good morning." Yesterday's magazine lady was back again. I wonder if she slept here too, like my mom had done again.

"Good morning," I answered, sliding the Munchkin box onto the counter. "Help yourself." She did. Two chocolate Munchkins and a bagel.

A cooking show was on the television without the volume—same as yesterday. Maybe that was comforting too? It didn't really do anything for me, but there were a few people in front of it this morning. For me, it was the fish tank. I looked for fish food before I sat down in front of it but didn't see any. I hoped it was someone's job to feed them. It seemed like a good question for Monica.

"T-Cell and Squamous."

"What?" I turned from the fish to see that a lanky kid had slipped into the chair next to mine. He looked like he was maybe fourteen.

"T-Cell and Squamous. The fish. That's what I call them. What do you call them?" He had a big smile, like Riley's but with crooked teeth. His pale-green T-shirt was not doing his complexion any favors. Or did everybody here eventually turn gray?

"AFib and P-SOCKS," I answered. "How did you know that I named the fish?"

"Everybody does," he answered. "I think it's a primal instinct for kids to name small animals in captivity."

"I'm not a kid," I shot back.

He ignored my protest. "What would you do if you found a pet hamster in here? I mean, you'd name it, wouldn't you?"

"I guess I would," I admitted. *I would name it Hermione,* I thought suddenly, without really thinking about it. So maybe it was a reflex more than an instinct.

"Jack."

"You would name a hamster Jack?"

"Me." He laughed. "My name is Jack."

"Nora."

"You or the imaginary hamster?"

"Me." I laughed. "Nora Reeves. The imaginary hamster is Hermione."

"Imaginary kitten?"

"Frances."

"Imaginary snake?"

"Voldemort. Too obvious, right? Let me try again. . . . Penelope."

"I'd love it if they had a snake in here. Wouldn't that be cool?"

"I don't think snakes are particularly calming. Fish are calming." Or so I had learned in the last twenty-four hours.

"There used to be three fish." He gestured toward the tank. "One of them died."

"I knew it!" I practically screeched, like I had just solved a murder.

"I scooped it out with a paper cup from the kitchen and flushed it."

The disgust must have been obvious on my face.

"What was I supposed to do? Leave it there to traumatize somebody? You can't have things alive one day and then dead the next. Definitely not in the PICU. Much better that it went missing." Okay, so this Jack kid was a mind reader. It was crazy.

"What was his name? The fish that died?"

"Chemo."

I stared blankly at him.

"Like Finding Chemo?"

I continued to stare.

"Chemotherapy? *Finding Nemo*?" He waited for me to get the joke. I didn't. "Well, I thought it was funny until he died. I never told my brother, though. That the fish died."

"Your brother?"

"Colin. He was actually okay with the name Chemo. It made him laugh."

"How old is your brother?"

"Seven. Leukemia."

"Leukemia?" I'd heard of that, but I wasn't really sure what it was. Jack the mind reader could tell, because he blurted out, "Cancer . . . in his blood cells.[22] How about you?"

"Huh?"

"Who are you visiting?"

"My cousin, Riley. She had a stroke."

"Ah, that explains the AFib and P-SOCKS." He pointed at the fish.

"You know those things?" Did he get a Monica welcome speech too?

"Yep."

---

[22] Leukemia is a cancer of the body's blood-forming tissues, including the bone marrow and lymphatic system, a system that helps rid the body of toxins.

"T-Cell and Squamous?" I asked. I did not know those things.

"T-Cell is a type of blood cell.[23] It's supposed to help you fight infection. Squamous[24] is just a shape of a cancer cell, really."

"You want a doughnut or something?" My knee-jerk reaction to pediatric cancer was apparently comfort food.

"Nah, I'm good. Doughnuts will kill you, you know. Poison for your body. Lots of chemicals." He didn't look like a doughnut eater, actually. Too skinny. He was also incredibly pale for the middle of July.

"You sound like my coach."

"Soccer?" he guessed.

"I run," I answered. "I just started last year. I'm pretty good, but not very fast, if that makes sense."

"Don't you have to be fast to be good?" We were looking at the fish tank, not each other.

"Not all the time," I answered. "It's cross-country—you know, long distance. It's different

---

[23] They are called T-cells because they mature in the thymus gland—a tiny gland between your lungs.

[24] Squamous technically means "covered in scales."

from running track. My best friend does it too. She's the one who convinced me to join." It felt weird to talk about myself in the middle of everything that was happening, but he sounded like he was interested. "I actually run better at courses with hills. Weird, right?"

"Sounds really . . . hard."

"Nah, it's all about endurance," I explained. It was true, too. I had faster times on hilly courses, even though Marisol is usually a better runner. "I'm supposed to be running all summer, at least three days a week, but, well, it's not important anymore."

"Why not?" he asked.

"Well, because." I hesitated. "We're here. Riley is important now." And Riley couldn't run. Or walk or talk or swallow. Or move all of her face.

"Jack?" Monica stuck her head in the doorway. So he *did* know Monica. "You have time for me this morning?"

"Sure." He stood up and shoved his hands in his pockets, suddenly looking uncomfortable. "See you later, Nora, AFib, P-SOCKS."

"Hi, Nora!" Monica waved. I waved back.

"See ya, Jack." I went back to watching the fish.

I should have asked which one was T-Cell and which one was Squamous.

The sickest I've ever been in my life was when I had the flu in the fourth grade. I had a 103 fever, and I did nothing for a full two days but sleep and sweat while my parents brought me toast and made me sip water. But on the third day, I suddenly felt a little better, maybe 50 percent myself, and my fever was gone. I sat up and asked for toast. On Riley's third day in the hospital, her second full day in the PICU, I was hoping for the stroke version of asking for toast. I went right to the sink to wash my hands before I even said hello—my number one responsibility as a Riley team member was not to spread germs.

"Good morning, Nora." Aunt Maureen smiled tiredly from her permanent spot next to Riley. "Look who's here, sweetheart." No response from Riley, or should I say the girl in the bed with the wires and the tubes and the numbers and the beeping who looked like a very bad flu version of Riley, without her voice or personality or funny eyebrow tricks. Like 20 percent Riley.

Beep beep beep.

"Hi, Riley," I said awkwardly in her direction and then smiled at my aunt, sitting down directly across from her. "My mom said she needs to make a few phone calls and then she is going to come up."

"Thanks, Nora," she answered. "How was the drive in today?"

"Not bad," I answered. "People were flying kites in some kind of park along the water. It was really cool."

"Sounds pretty," she answered absentmindedly. "Is it windy out today?"

"I didn't think so, but the kites were whipping around like crazy." Aunt Maureen hadn't been outside since she climbed into the back of the ambulance.

"That's right, not far from the bridge," she said, remembering. "I've seen them before. It's a great spot for kites because of the ocean breezes. We'll have to head over there when you get out of here, Riley." Riley wasn't looking at her mother. She seemed to be looking out into the hallway. Something about the angle of her head made the facial paralysis less noticeable.

Beep beep beep.

"Have you ever flown a kite?" Aunt Maureen asked.

I tried to remember a time that I had. "No, I don't think so."

"Really? My sister never took you kite flying?"

"Maybe I was too young to remember?" I had absolutely never flown a kite, but I didn't want to ruin the conversation.

"She should take you now. Well, not now exactly . . ."

"I know what you mean," I answered, glancing at Riley and then embarrassed that I had glanced at Riley. *Yes, tell your cousin she's the reason you can't fly a kite.*

"Once when I was little, younger than you, a kite actually picked me up off the ground! I was airborne! It was just a split second and I let go of the string, I was so scared!" Her face lit up as she thought about it. "Lost the stupid kite, but I never forgot the feeling!"

"I'd love to be airborne!"

"This summer," she said optimistically. "Riley and I are going to make sure you fly a kite this summer!"

Beep beep beep.

"Hi, guys! How's everybody today?" My mother bounced into the room, handing me coffee to hand over to her sister so she could wash her hands.

"Planning a trip to the park to fly kites," answered Aunt Maureen. "And we're not leaving until somebody's airborne!"

She winked at me and rubbed Riley's arm excitedly. She really was planning a kite outing in her head. She could see past 20 percent Riley. Hear something other than the *beep beep beep*. See a summer that might still have room for kites.

"Why don't you grab some breakfast, Nora? Your dad said that you didn't really eat this morning." My mother's hands were sufficiently clean, and the first thing she did was take one of Riley's in her own. "How are you today, sweetheart? How did you sleep?"

"Bye." I waved to Riley, shocked to find that she was looking at me and sort of suddenly expected a wave back. But not today. Today was not the day. Twenty percent Riley could almost make eye contact, did not speak, and might or might not be interested in kite flying. She definitely did not want toast.

Beep beep beep.

* * *

My visit done for the day, I headed back to the family room. With one entire wall of the room made of glass, it was easy to see who was in there and who was not. Now that I was on my third day here, I recognized some of the people as they came in. Lots of people fell asleep in here too, mostly by accident. Bags, books, and newspapers sometimes open on their laps. Heads back, mouths open. Everybody in varying states of shock, despite the comfort food and the fish tank.

I sat down facing the fish tank again and pulled a pink ottoman toward me with my foot, the screech made by its metal feet against the floor startling a middle-aged man napping in front of the television. He was asleep again before I could even apologize.

I tossed my backpack on the green-blue combo chair next to me, saving it for Jack, in case he showed up again. I pulled my summer homework packet out, and my runner's log came out with it. Running. Right. I was supposed to be running over the summer. I had managed to keep up a good streak at home, running two to three nonconsecutive days (okay, I ran too often), for thirty to forty minutes. The feelings column always made me laugh, because I wasn't sure how I was supposed to feel when I ran. I mean, what was I supposed to "feel" when I was running besides my legs, my breath, and my feet? I had even asked Riley if she wanted to run with me. She laughed out loud. She's not a runner. Three days later she couldn't walk or talk, let alone run. I had some feelings about *that*. I grabbed a green pen, the first one I could find:

Visitor's
~~Runner's~~ Log

Name:

DAY	DISTANCE	TYPE (trail, sidewalk, hills, etc)	FEELINGS	COMMENTS
7/1	2m	sidewalk		
7/3	1.5	sidewalk		
7/4	2	Track	Happy fourth!	
7/6	1	park		RAIN!!!
7/8	2.5	Track		with Mari
7/9	1	sidewalk	Excited!	driving to NY today!
7/11	1	sidewalk		Riley refuses to run! BOO!
today	15min	P.I.C.U.		
yesterday	15min	P.I.C.U.		Beep, Beep.
??	—	E.R.	—	—

"Jeez, how much homework did your school give you? It's summer!" Jack appeared silently, this time with a cup of black coffee in his hand. He looked slightly less gray than he had earlier.

"This? This isn't homework. Well, it was, sort of . . . ," I trailed off, and slid my runner's/visitor's log beneath the summer math packet on my lap. "I had a summer essay to do . . . but . . . I did most of it already." What was I supposed to do with my essay now, give it a horrible surprise ending?

He leaned over for a look at the math. "Decimals?"

"Yeah, I could actually use some help with decimals." I actually didn't mind the math. It would give me something to do besides watch the fish and the muted cooking shows.

"Decimals aren't really my strong point," he confessed.

"Don't you have summer homework too?"

"Nope."

"I thought summer homework was universal. Like fish naming."

He smiled. "I'm excused . . . because of my brother . . . because of this. . . . You could probably get excused too."

"I don't want to be excused. That's just lazy."
Jack took it like a slap. "Oh gosh, that didn't come
out right," I backtracked. "I meant for *me*. You
should be excused . . . I'm sorry. How's Colin?"
Now I slid the homework packet beneath the
runner's/visitor's log, embarrassed.

"Same. Riley?" He was moving on from my
faux pas. I couldn't believe I'd said something so
stupid.

"Same."

"I think I saw her," he said, sipping his coffee
in between bites of a strip of beef jerky.

"But how did you know . . ."

"I kind of keep track of who comes and goes,"
he answered. "You guys don't look anything alike.
You're cousins?"

"Yeah, my mom and her mom are sisters."

"I guess you guys are close?"

"Yeah," I answered. "I mean we don't see each
every day because I live in Maryland, but, yeah,
we're close. . . ." *She has a secret boyfriend she
never told me about, and she hit me the night
before she had a stroke, but yeah, we're close.*

"You drove up when she got sick? That's cool.

We used to have a lot of family visitors—aunts, uncles, you name it. Then it kind of petered out as things, well, dragged on." I suddenly realized I hadn't seen him in the family room *with* anyone. I was here on my own a lot too, sure, but I hadn't seen him with any other adult besides Monica. Where were his parents?

But what I said was, "No, we were already here . . . at Coney Island . . . at the amusement park, when it happened."

"Your cousin had a stroke at the amusement park?" I hadn't put it in a sentence before. It was a terrible sentence, and even though there was nothing new in it, hearing it out loud was awful. *My cousin had a stroke at the amusement park.*

"Yeah." I didn't offer any details.

"I walk down there sometimes, from here. I went more before it got so hot. In May it was great—and hardly anyone there. But now the sun is brutal."

I did a quick calculation. "Colin's been here since May?" Two months was a long time to be in the hospital.

"More or less, yeah. Not always in the PICU." Hospital lingo.

"Oh." I thought intensive care was the only place you could be with cancer. He didn't say anything more about Colin. We weren't really big on swapping medical details. "Are your mom and dad here too?"

"My dad doesn't come anymore. And my mom's at work. No work, no health insurance. You know." I didn't know. There were so many people in and out of the family room that I just assumed *everybody* stopped going to work when bad things happened. Mom and Dad and Aunt Maureen had stopped going to work. I didn't know some people could and some people couldn't. There was an awkward silence.

"Have you ever actually *seen* anybody feed the fish? P-SOCKS looks a little off." The fish did seem a little wobbly to me.

"He's blue," he said, pointing out the obvious. "It's tough to look healthy when you're blue."

"Maybe that's how Chemo died? Maybe nobody fed him?" I was suddenly concerned that there *really* wasn't anybody feeding the fish.

"I don't know. They run a pretty tight ship around here. I'm fairly confident they make sure the fish get fed. Seems like a no-brainer."

"Well, if something is going to slip through the cracks, it may as well be the fish."

He laughed, but only a little. Possibly a tomato-soup laugh.

"What's that?" He pointed at my lap, where my runner's log was hanging over the side, threatening to slip to the floor.

I shrugged. "It's just a stupid thing I did. . . . I was . . . bored." I hurried to put the runner's/visitor's log away, but he stopped me.

"Come on, let me see? Please?" He must have been pretty desperate for something to do.

"Um, sure."

It didn't take long for a reaction, but it wasn't the one I expected.

"They only let you see her once a day? For fifteen minutes?" Jack sounded like he was going to march off to Monica and demand more time for me.

"Well, no. It's not that, it's, you know, it's just kind of hard to see her with all the tubes and stuff." I was completely flustered. "So we decided that I would just go once a day."

"Oh. Sounds . . . easier." Monica was no longer his target, and his face was gaining color rapidly.

"No! Not easier. Monica said I could decide and that it was important for me to, you know, have a choice. . . ." It *was* Monica's suggestion, after all. And she *was* a specialist. "Plus, you know, she can't even talk and she's mostly asleep." The more I said, the worse I sounded.

"'Beep, beep'?" he read from my comments. "Interesting."

I snatched the runner's log out of his hands but refused to look at him. "I have homework to do."

"Yeah," Jack stood up. "No excuses, right?" I didn't look up. "See ya later."

I didn't see Jack again that afternoon. I guess he hung out with his brother the rest of the day. By lunchtime, I had finished decimals, compared rational numbers, and wrapped up the whole summer's worth of improper fractions.

When I was done, I did a few casual loops around the floor to see if I could find Jack, but it's hard to look around without staring into patients' rooms, and that is just not something you do. Even though we were all there together, in the family room and the elevators and the hallways, sharing small talk and doughnuts and magazines, the patients' wide-open glass cubes where families sat and slept and cried and waited were the most private of places. They were where you pretended not to see.

A few hours later my mother and father walked into the family room with an announcement.

"I'm going back to the house with you today." Apparently it was more of an order from Aunt Maureen than a decision Mom had made, but for at least one night, Mom was leaving the hospital. I was practically giddy when I slid into the backseat of the car and Mom got in the passenger seat in the front. It was the first normal thing that had happened since they lowered the safety bar on the roller coaster.

"You're making a big difference, Nora," Mom told me as soon as her seat belt clicked. "It's great that you sit with Riley. It helps her more than you can tell. And I know it must be hard. It helps Aunt Maureen, too." Truth: I had been feeling pretty lousy about my fifteen minutes a day since my conversation with Jack, and Mom exaggerating how much it was helping made me suspicious.

"When will she be . . . you know, better?" *When will she sit up and ask for toast? When will she be able to talk? When will the stroke be* over? I watched the exit signs glow in the headlights.

"Everything takes time," she answered, pulling her hair out of its ponytail. And wow, my mom had a serious case of hospital hair. I felt my own greasy hair and then wiped my hands on the seat. I wondered if Mom was going to jump right into a shower when we got back to the house—or if she even cared at all what she looked like. "She's certainly better than she was four days ago."

"How do you know? I mean, her vitals[25] are always the same. I always check, and they haven't really changed. What should the numbers be?"

"Her vitals are good. That's why there's no change. She's stable."

"If she's stable, then why is she still in intensive care?" What use were the numbers then? Why have them blink at you all day if they didn't change anything?

"I'm—I'm not sure," Mom stammered. She shot

[25] As a reminder, vitals are temperature, HR, RES, BP, and P-SOCKS.

a look to my dad, and I worried that she was going to change her mind about coming back to the house.

"Actually, it's the very small things that tell you someone is getting better," Dad explained. Mom seemed to relax when he took over the conversation. "And then the small things get a little bigger. Today she was awake a bit more, and she pointed at the water pitcher when she was thirsty. Those are good things."

I thought about what Aunt Mo had said about her brain sparking. "Like sparks?" I also thought about how I hadn't seen a single spark myself.

"Sort of . . . yes. Sparks."

"So how many sparks did you see today?"

"How many? I'm not sure . . . ," answered Mom. "Her eye crinkled up when Aunt Maureen came back into the room."

"Does that really mean something?" It didn't seem like much. "Anything else?"

"She repeated some sounds today when your aunt was talking to her," said my dad.

"What sounds?" I took the runner's/visitor's log out of my backpack. If sparks = progress, then I could actually keep track of them. Ugh. The log was a confused mess. I turned the paper over and scribbled *SPARKS* across the top of it, then made a tally mark.

"I couldn't really make them out," he answered. "But Aunt Maureen seemed to understand them." I erased the tally mark I had just made. But the water pitcher? That was a good one. I wished I had been there to see it. I made two tally marks, one for recognizing the water pitcher and one for knowing to point at it. Did Colin spark for Jack? I'm sure he did. But was that the type of thing Jack looked for when he visited? We weren't just looking for progress, we were expecting it. Was Jack?

"Does she spark when you go in the room, Mom?" I was pretty sure *I* didn't generate any sparks for her.

"I think . . . so," Mom said, then yawned. Her head was against the window. I wanted to talk more about sparks, but I knew how tired she was. A few seconds later there was light snoring from the front seat. I studied my two sad little tally marks. Three days in the hospital and Riley could point to a water pitcher. Was that ever going to add up to anything?

* * *

When we got home, Archie was waiting at the door, as always. His barking was less maniacal—he finally trusted that we were coming back for him. Plus, one of the neighbors came during the day to take him for a walk.

"I'll bring him out back, Dad," I offered. "Come on, boy." I patted my leg and he followed me through the kitchen and out the screen door, making a beeline to the dark part of the yard to take care of business. When he came back, he sat in front of me and began to whine. If Archie had the chance, he would visit Riley in a heartbeat and stay by her side all day long. If he was a normal-size dog, I swear I would smuggle him in to see her. Riley would love that! I reached for the door, but he didn't follow me. Instead he sat by the gate, looking out toward the street. Waiting for Riley, I was certain.

"Come on, Archie," I said, patting my leg again. "Come on!"

He ignored me.

"Riley will be home! Yes, she will!" I used the singsongy dog voice Riley used when she was talking to him. I felt like an idiot, really, but he was acknowledging me now—listening. He really was. "She misses you! And when she sees you again, you are gonna get the biggest spark ever!" He barked at me and wagged his tail, following me at last back into the house and up to Riley's room. Dog language. I didn't even know I could speak it.

Up in her room, we both headed for the same thing—the smell of Riley's coconut shampoo on her pillow. He beat me to it. All I could think about when spread out on the cool sheets, fan blowing on my face, was that I had just spent more time talking to the dog than I had spent talking to Riley since she'd been in the hospital.

Jack was right. There really was no excuse for me.

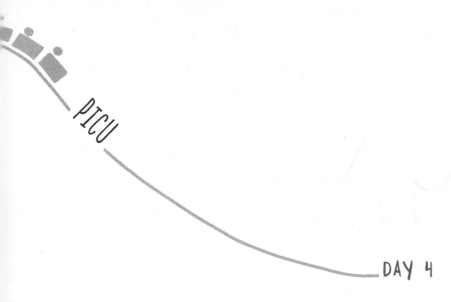

PICU

DAY 4

S o, do you talk *to* Riley when you're in the room?"
I asked as I plopped down at the kitchen table for
breakfast and my mother handed me a sandwich.
She'd gotten some sleep, taken a shower, and she
looked—and smelled—like Mom again.

"Great news!" she announced, ignoring my
question. "Aunt Mo texted me first thing this
morning—Riley's been upgraded from critical condition to serious!

"That's great!" I tried to match the enthusiasm
in her voice, but I wasn't exactly sure what it meant.
I mean, "serious" doesn't sound too hot either. I had
already decided—as I was falling asleep last night—
that I was going to go see Riley more than once a

93

day. Two times, definitely, or maybe even three. I wanted to see sparks for myself. I wanted to *bring* Riley a spark, if I could. I know it would sound like I was only more comfortable going because she wasn't in critical condition anymore . . . but the lousy truth was I had barely seen her. Sixty minutes total, and that was counting the few minutes in the ER and the time I spent with Dad in the hallway watching Aunt Mo and Riley. I couldn't bring myself to put that on the log, but I was counting it in my head. She had gone from critical to serious, and I pretty much had absolutely nothing to do with it. I was the weak link on the team and I wanted to do a better job. I wanted to be a part of her recovery.

I opened up the turkey sandwich and peeled off the lettuce. That was breakfast this morning, because there wasn't much else in the house besides cold cuts and pasta. The neighbors kept the fridge stuffed with good, solid dinner food. Froot Loops were not on the list.

"I'm asking your dad to pick up a fruit salad for the hospital," she said without looking up. She was texting him on his morning run to the bagel store/bakery and now grocery.

"And Froot Loops," I added. "Can you ask him to get Froot Loops?"

"And Froot Loops," she repeated as she typed it into her phone.

"So, Riley?" Mom stared at me.

"Do you talk *to* her when you're in the room?" I repeated. "Do you sorta pretend that Riley can answer you?"

"I guess I just talk." My mom paused to think. "Her speech therapist encouraged us to engage with Riley as much as we can. Get her to process language, even if she's not ready to answer us. So, I guess Maureen and I talk a lot to each other and we just try to include her." She picked the lettuce off the table and pushed the mayonnaise my way. "It's still good for her to hear about real things and real life. It's a good exercise for her brain to focus and listen."

"Okay, but there is no real life here," I said. Mom frowned at me. "I didn't mean it like that." I smeared mayonnaise all over the sandwich and then squished the top piece of bread back on. Mayonnaise oozed out the sides. My mom is completely grossed out by mayonnaise, so I put the lid back on quickly.

"I know this is hard, honey. Just, you know, talk about whatever you guys talk about." The lid wasn't enough distance between my mom and mayonnaise, so she got up and put it back in the fridge. "School? Archie? Boys?"

"Boys?" I cringed. "We don't talk about boys!" Partial lie. We didn't *talk* about boys. But we did have a fight about *one* boy. A big fight.

A phone-cracking fight about a secret boy with a code name.

 GEORGINA

I stuffed way too much sandwich in my mouth and had to spit some back out on the plate.

"Okay, that was gross." She stared at me a little too long. "Well, then, how about you talk about other things that interest her?"

"I just can't think of anything." My stomach was twisting in knots. So far all I had was *Hi, Riley. I'm sorry you had a stroke. Today I had mayonnaise for breakfast. Do you like mayonnaise, Riley? Or would you like to talk about music or secret boyfriends?* I ate my sandwich to the crusts and then built a bread frame out of them.

My mom grabbed a corner of the one mayonnaise-free crust and popped it in her mouth. I hadn't seen her eat anything else for breakfast. I thought about what Monica had said about families needing to eat and offered her the rest of my crust. She cringed. Stupid mayo. "It will feel funny, I get that. I really do. It's hard to talk to somebody who can't talk back," she said. "But it's important to try."

"Is anybody else going to come visit her? Like her friends? Where are they?"

"Maureen said Riley doesn't want them to," answered Mom. "At least not yet." It's one thing to point at the water pitcher when you're thirsty, but how in the world could Riley have told her mother she didn't want her friends to visit her? Aunt Mo was either really, really good at communicating with Riley or she was really, really good at imagining it.

"But it would be good for her, wouldn't it?"

"I think that's Riley's decision. Maybe when she feels better."

"Okay, Mom," I said. "I'll figure something out." I gave the last bit of crust to Archie, who was sitting under the table, waiting for it. He gobbled it up and then licked my toes. Ewwww! I was disgusted but laughed anyway. That's what the PICU needed, I thought, a dog! Although maybe not one quite so . . . Archie. Jack would love it, although he'd probably name it a medical term I'd never heard of, and he'd probably feed it coffee and beef jerky.

"I'm going to make another sandwich," I told my mother.

"For later?"

"For Jack, my friend at the hospital. I'm not sure he eats enough." Should I make one for Colin, too? I wasn't sure if he could eat solid food, but I didn't want Jack to think that I had forgotten about him. I made two.

"We're leaving in fifteen minutes," Dad announced from the front door. "And I have enough fruit salad to feed ten people!"

A sandwich in each hand, I took the stairs two at a time to get my backpack and load it up for the day. I put the sandwiches down on the bed—and then caught Archie very clearly hatching his own plan for them.

"Nice try, bud!" I moved them up to the bookshelf—about the only place he wouldn't be able to reach. I ran my finger over Riley's name, scratched into the purple paint. Then I saw them. Right above her name were exactly what I needed— her favorite books. Nope, not the ones that are probably your favorites. Riley's were . . . wait for it . . . presidential biographies. See? Probably not on your list. Not just the major presidents who everybody knows, either, like Washington and Lincoln (her personal favorite), but the ones nobody ever talks about, like Ulysses S. Grant and Calvin Coolidge. The books were old and heavy, like textbooks, but Riley's had them since she was in the second grade. Her dad had gotten the whole set for her at a garage sale, and he used to read them out loud to her. I could maybe read to her about presidents! It might even get me a spark!

I scanned the titles until I saw Abraham Lincoln and remembered an afternoon when Riley decided that I, too, needed to know all about him. I'd *uh-huh*'d for an hour. Yeah, it's weird.[26] I know.

I took Ol' Abe's biography off the shelf and slid it into my backpack, followed by the sandwiches.

---

[26] And not the stuff anybody knows.

Then, at the last minute, I grabbed one of Riley's sketchbooks, some colored pencils, and even her pillowcase off the pillow and shoved those in there too. Maybe stuff from her room would spark her.

As I put on my sneakers, Archie positioned himself to jump on the bed with me. I closed my hand into a fist and held it over his head. *Sit,* I hand-said, using Riley's closed-fist hand signal. He sat. *Stay,* I hand-said, holding my palm flat and my fingers up. He stayed.

Archie stared at me. Waiting for more words? "She'll be back, boy." Archie huffed and lowered his head to the floor. *He smells tomato soup,* I thought. I took Riley's pillowcase out of my back-pack and put it back on the bed for Archie—after I took a sniff of it myself. I think he needed it more than Riley did.

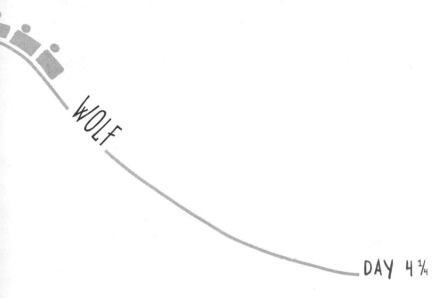

DAY 4 ¾

Of course, it started pouring as we drove to the hospital, and the parking lot, of course, was full, so we had to park a few blocks away and I'd clearly jammed way too much in my backpack, which was getting wetter and heavier by the block. I worried the stuff in there was getting ruined. I should have wrapped it all in a plastic bag. Riley's sketchbook was in there too! Shoot! That would be a great conversation starter, wouldn't it? _Hey, I brought all this stuff that is important and highly personal to you and then took a walk in the rain! Look how charcoal pencil drawings run when they're wet!_

Dad was none too pleased either, working hard to keep his bagels, doughnuts, pastries, and fruit

101

salad from getting drenched. He really had bought enough for a party.

In the family room, while Mom did her morning check-in with Aunt Mo, and Dad muttered about wet bags and poor packing in the kitchen, I unzipped the backpack and pulled out the sketchbook. Phew, it was dry . . . just one corner a teensy bit discolored. Something I haven't mentioned yet is that Riley was a real artist. She could draw just about anything— giraffes, owls, cheetahs, or even dragons and castles. I found the page with her wolf. Riley's wolves were great. This is the wolf she tried to teach me to draw the day before we went to Coney Island:

"You claim to be a runner, but every time I see you, you're sitting." Jack was back, in the same clothes he wore yesterday.

"Did you sleep here?" Sleeping here was not good. You slept here when the third thing was possible.

"Nope. Why?"

Because you look tired and you're wearing the same clothes. I thought better of it. "No reason. Here, I brought you a sandwich. Colin, too. Hope you like turkey . . . and mayo."

"Wow. Thank you." He looked like he was about to say more, but changed his mind, unwrapping one sandwich immediately. He devoured half of it and carried the other half to the kitchen, smiling at the magazine lady in her usual spot. "Seriously, you shouldn't sit all day. They say sitting is as bad as smoking."

"They do not."

"They do."

"I can't run. Where am I supposed to run?"

"Run the stairs. Some of the neurology nurses do it before shift on Tuesdays and Thursdays." Jack popped one of the little cup things into the coffee-maker and began rummaging around in a cabinet above the microwave while his cup brewed.

"Jeez, you really have been here too long!" *Shoot!* It's like I saved up every stupid thing I could say until I got to the family room—and then I spilled them all over the floor.

"You got that right." Jack let me off the hook

again. Why did he do that? He was clearly much nicer than me. "Running stairs is really good for your heart—and your legs. You'll have monstrous legs, like tree trunks."

"Sounds . . . comfortable." He laughed harder than I expected, and then I did too.

"Seriously, you're going to lose your mind if you sit all day," Jack went on as he did a lap around my chair, half a sandwich in one hand, his fresh coffee in the other.

"I'm a cross-country runner," I argued, "not an up-and-down-the-stairs runner." He widened the circle, lapping around both chairs.

"Stairs are like hills. Plus, seems to me if you really wanted to run, you'd run where you can. What does the direction matter?"[27] I stuck one leg straight out in front of me to prevent another go-around. He was about to step over it when the wolf caught his attention.

"Nice!" he said. "Did you do that?" Finally, sitting.

---

[27] I think it does matter, because you use different muscles, and vertical running is tougher on your heart (cardiovascular) and lungs (respiratory). Not to mention your glutes (butt).

"Uh . . . I don't really do animals," I said. "Riley did it. But she did *try* to teach me. I'll show you how good I am." I turned to my version on the next page:

"Whoa," he said without skipping a beat, "that is not good. Have you ever even seen a wolf?" He picked up the remote and aimed it at the TV. "I'm sure we can find one for you on the Discovery Channel—"

"Riley made me draw it with my eyes closed!" I explained. "She told me to picture a wolf in my head, then draw what I saw."

"Is that how you see a wolf? It looks like a pig with a straw coming out of its eye."

"You try it, then!" I grabbed a pen from my backpack and shoved it toward him. Then I repeated what Riley had told me. "Picture a wolf in your head and send the thought down your arm." He followed the instructions and then showed me this:

"Okay, *that* looks like a rabbit in a bow tie."

"Better than the straw pig."

"Is not."

"Is."

"Is not!" Some new people came in—newbies were pretty easy to spot—and Jack and I instantly lowered our voices. "Anyway, Riley said the point was to try to get you to see the wolf in a different way." Persistent as always. But Riley hadn't stopped there—or given up on my weird pig-wolf with an eye straw. She'd sat beside me and showed me step by step. We'd erased. We'd started over. I copied what Riley did. To remind you, the Riley wolf was this:

Then, one step at a time, Riley walked me to the wolf. It wasn't perfect, but in less than an hour, Riley had taken me from

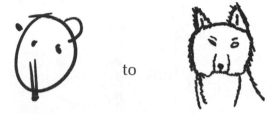

to

I showed Jack. "Hey," he said, putting his coffee down and taking the book from my hands, genuinely impressed. "That's amazing. It actually looks like a wolf."

"Yep," I said. "Riley showed me step by step. The loose lines for fur, the eyes slanted a bit. The ears and the snout. She would draw and explain and I would copy it. Face, fur, eyes, snout, ears. Trust me, it took a while."

He turned the pages to admire more of Riley's work. Then he paused at one page. "Uh-oh—I guess she didn't enjoy the Cyclone too much, huh?"

"What?" My chest instantly tightened, like someone had grabbed me by the lungs. "What are you talking about?"

He turned the sketchbook around to show me.

I glanced nervously at Jack. Riley even looked scared in the drawing. Bug-eyed and openmouthed. "The—the night before—" I stuttered. "She—she—must have sketched it while I was out for a run or something." Hot tears sprang to my eyes, and I finally snatched the sketchbook from Jack and tore the drawing out.

"Okay then." Jack was looking at me funny. A prolonged-eye-contact child-life-specialist kind of look. "That's it, right? That's when—" That mind-reading thing again.

"Nora?" Dad stood in the doorway. "You ready to go?"

"Be right there," I said, jamming the roller-coaster

page into my backpack and then spending entirely too much time zipping and unzipping every compartment like I needed to find something specific. "I just need . . . I mean, I'm just looking for . . ."

"Everything okay?"

Jack stood up and walked toward him, introducing himself and buying me time. "Hi, Mr. Reeves, I'm Jack."

"Nice to meet you, Jack," Dad answered, taking his eyes off me. "I hear you guys have been keeping each other company."

"Yeah, absolutely," he replied. "How's Riley?"

"She's good," Dad answered. "Getting better." Dad was in full small-talk mode now and kept going. Jack was clearly a pro at this. He bought me at least three minutes. I took a few deep breaths and got myself together.

"Ready, Dad. See you later, Jack."

"Later. Thanks for the sandwiches. Next time, more mayo?"

Make small talk, I reminded myself as I walked toward Riley's room, sketchbook in hand. *Include Riley. Talk about the wolf. Look, Aunt Mo, I brought some of Riley's drawings from home. Don't forget to include Riley. Give her time to answer you, even though she won't actually answer you. Do you remember the wolf we did together?*

"Hands." My dad prodded me toward the sink as my mother excused herself to abide by the visiting rules.

"Huh? Oh, right. Sorry. Hands." I held the book between my knees while I soaped and rinsed. Hands washed, standing next to Riley's bed, I took a deep breath. Riley's eyes were already on me. She half smiled at me and raised her hand, like a small wave! SPARK! She looked different too. Was she missing a tube? *One* tube? She was; there had been a tube taped down to the side of her mouth, hadn't there? Or was it her lips? Her lips, of all things, looked . . . better . . . normal. Less chapped and dry and split. Lips for talking, not lips for a tube.

"Did you want to show us something?" Aunt Mo encouraged me, pointing at the sketchbook.

"Um . . . yeah. Right. I found this wolf sketch that you did. It's . . . really good . . . and I just thought I would show it to you." I opened the sketchbook. Riley was still watching me, so I said, "Do you remember when we—"

"Excuse me." A nurse appeared and checked some of the equipment and numbers. Another false start. *Grrrr.* The nurse tapped away at the computer that seemed to be at the center of it all. We stepped out of his way, and I realized that I was still standing there like a human easel with the wolf picture on display. The nurse left without saying anything else.

"That's a great picture, honey." Aunt Mo motioned me closer to Riley. "Bring it here so Riley can see it better."

I took a step closer. Riley pursed her lips a few times and muttered some sounds I couldn't understand. I came even closer and put the sketchbook on the tray in front of her. "Do you remember? We worked on this last week? You showed me how to draw it too." Riley scanned it with her eyes and then looked up at her mother, not at me. Aunt Mo gave me a small nod to continue. I loved Aunt Mo so much for giving me cues. I turned the page and pointed to my wolf.

"You taught me how to draw a wolf," I repeated, slower this time. I flipped back to my original wolf. "My first one looked like this."

"Oh my," Aunt Maureen said politely.

A sound, like a grunt, leaked out of Riley. *Was that a laugh?*

"Riley, do you remember this?" Aunt Mo asked, excitedly pointing at my pig straw wolf. She was talking to Riley like she always did—like Riley was going to answer. I guess that was the right way. I would do that too. Riley reached toward the wolf.

"That was the first one," I said, glancing at Aunt

Mo. "Riley told me to draw it with my eyes closed." She looked from me to Riley, tilting her head toward my cousin in a sit-beside-her kind of way. I sat down in the chair next to Riley. "My wolf was terrible, and you helped me. You told me to draw it with my eyes closed." I tried to keep eye contact with Riley without giving her that *concerned* eye contact that I hated and was sure she would too. Riley stared at the page for a long time. "See?" I said. "It looks like a pig with a straw. Well, it sort of does, but my friend tried—" My father put his hand on my shoulder. *Wait.* I think that's what Dad meant. Wait for Riley.

After she had looked at it for a while, I turned to the page with her wolf. "This is your wolf, Riley. It's amazing."

Riley studied it for a full minute while we waited. She finally raised her eyes slowly off the page and up to me. The outer corner of her left eye still drooped, giving it a different shape than her right one. But it was much better than a few days ago. I managed to hold her gaze for a few seconds, but then I had to look away because looking had started to feel too much like *staring*. Riley lowered her eyes again and ran her hand over the page, rubbing her finger over the top where the corner was damp from the rain. I knew I should have protected it better! She flattened her fingers across the picture and then flicked the edge of the page with her thumb, snapping it. *Snap, snap, snap, snap, snap.*

"It's yours," I said. "Your sketchbook. I brought it from your room." I pulled the chair closer to the bed. Could she even understand me? "I can show—" I stopped and looked at my aunt. She nodded. I leaned over Riley's weak arm. "I can show you more. . . ." Riley flattened her hand, covering the wolf entirely. Again she pursed her lips, over and over. Did it mean something? It must. I just didn't know what, so I didn't know what to say. "Mmmmmm," she hummed. "Mmmmm??"

I looked at Aunt Mo. *Me?* Was she saying *me?* *It sounded like a question,* I thought. That was a spark too, wasn't it? Knowing how to make your word sound like a question? Riley leaned back against her pillow and closed her eyes, her hand still resting on top of the wolf.

"Are there more sketches in there, Nora? Can I see?" Aunt Maureen took the book from the table. I relaxed back into the chair, relieved—I'm so awful, but I *was*—Aunt Maureen was taking over, but also feeling like I had done okay. Like Riley had recognized the wolf.

Aunt Maureen leafed through the sketchbook, smiling. I thought she was going to show the pages to Riley, but she kept flipping through the sketchbook again and again.

"You've been drawing and sketching since you were big enough to hold a pencil," she said at last. She rolled the tray table away and sat on the bed, turning the pages, showing Riley, teaching Riley more about being Riley. "Don't ask me where you got it from either," she said with a laugh. "I can't draw worth a lick and neither can anyone else in the family." Actually, I knew that wasn't true. Uncle Pete was a pretty good artist. He used to draw stories for Riley. I've seen them. I checked Riley's face for some kind of protest, but there was nothing there.

"You ready for me?" A woman I hadn't seen before walked in with a large canvas tote bag on her shoulder. "I'm sorry to interrupt." She smiled at Riley first and then addressed Aunt Maureen. "How's everybody today?"

"Good," replied Aunt Maureen enthusiastically. "I guess it's talking time!"

"Huh?" I asked.

"Speech therapy," explained the woman. "I'm Josephine, Riley's speech therapist.[28] Now that she's feeling better, she gets to spend more time with me!" She took some charts out of her tote and rolled the table back in front of Riley.

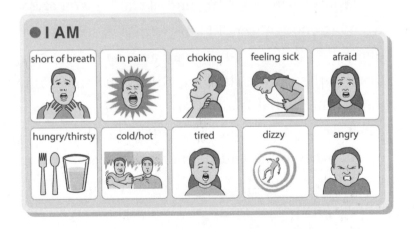

---

[28] Speech therapists don't just work on speech! They also help patients practice swallowing. Same part of brain! See diagram.

Fake half smile. No eye crinkle. Tomato-soup smile? Not sure Riley enjoyed her speech therapy or the charts.

"Thank you for bringing this in, Nora," Aunt Mo said to me, closing the book and handing it back. "That was a real treat! Don't you think so, Riley?" Riley waved her fingers again. Agreement? Or was I catching Aunt Maureen's imaginary spark bug?

"Sure, no problem." I smiled at Aunt Mo and wedged the sketchbook into my backpack. "I'll see you guys later. Bye, Riley." Half smile. *Some crinkling! A spark for me!*

"Mmmmm," Riley said, exaggerating her closed lips for the *M* sound. A long humming sound. "Mmmmooo."[29] I stopped what I was doing. Riley stared and blinked. "Moo," she said again. "Moo." Riley jerked her hand back. Her left hand. Her weak hand. I hadn't seen it move yet. I jumped, but Aunt Mo didn't. She leaned in closer.

"Moo?" repeated Aunt Mo.

"Keep going, Riley, tell us more." Josephine was leaning forward, encouraging Riley to continue. Riley's arm jerked again, striking Aunt Maureen in the side of the face. This time she jumped too. Riley's face twisted, her hand stuck in Aunt Maureen's curls—as crazy and big as Riley's own hair. She pulled Aunt Maureen's head roughly toward her.

"Ooh, girl, you are getting strong!" Aunt Maureen laughed, and buried her own hand in her mass of curls, wrapping it right over Riley's.

"Moo-Moo," said Riley. "Moo-Moo."

---

[29] Interesting side note: The reason so many different languages have an *M* word for mother is because *Mmmm* is often the first sound a baby makes, accidentally, by humming!

"Moo-Moo is Mom," Josephine surmised. "Is that right, Riley?"

"Moo-Moo," repeated Riley. One eye crinkled. "Moo-Moo." Aunt Maureen grabbed Riley's face in both hands and covered her face in kisses.

Spark. Spark. Spark.

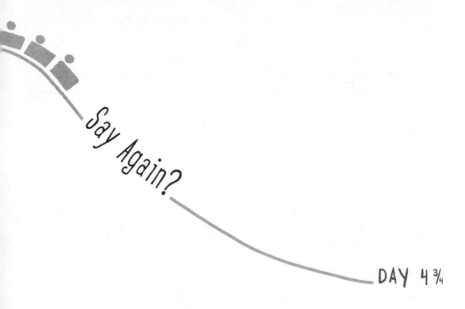

Say Again?

So you're saying that if Riley can't read, she's supposed to know that this means father? Really? Does this look like anybody's dad?"

Father

"If you have a comic-book dad." Jack and I both laughed. I had told Jack about Riley's word chart[30] that morning, and by lunchtime he had a stack of them from Monica.

[30] These charts can be extremely helpful, and I am not trying to make anyone feel bad about the drawings! I am sure it is also way better to use one with a professional speech therapist than with two tired, snarky kids in the PICU family room.

"And *this* means Mom?" I asked.

"I guess so? But it could mean baby or doctor, or women or . . . feminism."

"Feminism?" I laughed. "Really? Who wakes up in a hospital and asks for feminism?"

"I would, for sure." Straight-faced. Jack was ridiculous.

I covered up the words under another picture and asked Jack what he thought it meant:

"Ice cream?" he guessed.

"Nope," I said, shaking my head. "Daughter."

"Daughter? Hmmm . . . I was going to say 'lick.' Although 'lick' is not really a hospital word." He stuck out his tongue with a *blech*. Although actually, I thought Riley was more likely to use the word "lick" in a sentence than some of the other words on the chart, like "bedpan."

"How about this one?" I tried.

"Old." I wasn't sure if he was kidding or not.

"Nope."

"Rocking chair," he tried again.

"Relaxed," I explained. "It means 'relaxed.'"

"Yeah, lots of relaxing in a hospital," he scoffed. The conversations I had with Jack were completely different from the conversations I had with Aunt Maureen, but what they did have in common was *not* a lot of medical talk. I didn't ask specifics about Colin's condition or prognosis unless Jack brought it up, and he was the same about Riley.

"I guess there's no 'cousin' on the board, huh?"

"Nope. No 'friend,' either, but that would be too hard, because what would a one-size-fits-all friend look like?" I asked. "I mean, a pillow is a pillow, but what does a generic friend look like?"

"I'm pretty generic—they could use my face."

"You're not generic." I laughed. "You're too tall to be generic."

"That's it? That's what makes me not generic— I'm too tall?" He pretended to be offended.

"Sorry, it's the first thing that popped into my head." Actually, Jack wasn't generic because I knew him a little bit now—and because his brother had cancer. There was nothing generic about that, but it's not something you can draw.

"She does have her own word for her mother," I explained. "It's Moo-Moo."

"Moo-Moo?"

"Yeah, she said it this morning. She said 'Moo-Moo' while she was grabbing my aunt. The beginning sound is right, so that's actually really good. Her name is Maureen, so she could be trying to say Mom or Maureen or even Mo, which is my aunt's nickname."

"Colin calls me Jax," explained Jack. "Or sometimes JackAttack. I call him Colon sometimes—the large intestine, not the punctuation."

"Goes without saying!" I laughed.

"So why don't you use Riley's word on the chart?"

"I don't get it."

"Cross out 'mother' under the picture and write 'Moo-Moo.'" He took a pen and did exactly that.

"Not a bad idea, Jack." It felt like a very good idea, actually. "But I don't think she'll make a connection between Moo-Moo and that drawing."

"So draw a new one," he said, looking suddenly doubtful, "or some kind of abstract version of your aunt, anyway. And *don't* do it with your eyes closed, like you did with the wolf. That is not going to be pretty."

I was already digging for a pen. "That's a great idea!" I wasn't the artist that Riley was (is? will be?), but maybe if I could make the pictures more recognizable, that might help her communicate!

I felt kind of giddy, imagining sparks galore. I closed my eyes and pictured Riley when she was just fine. Her dark eyes, swinging ponytail, and earrings, always earrings (like her mom, I supposed). I drew her on a blank page of Riley's sketchbook.

Aunt Maureen was next. Even in my cartoon-like sketches, there was a definite resemblance between mother and daughter.

My dad (Uncle Mike to Riley).

My mom (Aunt Paige to Riley). (I decided to give everybody regular-life hair, not hospital hair.)

The dog. Of course, I kind of pictured Archie in my head like this:

But I drew him like this:

Jack took it all in. "Not bad. But where's Riley's father?" Jack looked at me. "Does she have one?" Good question. Did she anymore?

"I'm not really sure. I mean, she has one, somewhere, I guess, but she hasn't seen him in a few years."

"That doesn't mean she doesn't want to talk about him." Jack stood up abruptly and made a beeline for the water cooler. The pale-green shirt was back—but he smelled like Tide, so at least it was clean. He filled a cup at the water cooler, sucked it down, and filled another before coming back over.

"Don't forget to draw yourself," he said, relaxed again. If there had been a moment to ask about his father, it had passed.

"She can just point to me," I said.

"What if she wants to talk about you when you're not there? Isn't that when you do the most talking about other people—when they're not in the room?" My heart skipped a beat. Riley might actually have plenty to say about me when I wasn't in the room. I wasn't sure I wanted to help her with that.

"Want me to do it?" he offered.

"Can you draw?" I asked suspiciously.

"Not at all," he declared, without a hint of embarrassment.

"I'll do it myself." Picturing my own face was really hard, but I gave it a shot. I thought I looked pretty random, but hoped the braid might be enough to make me recognizable, at least to Riley. For the record, I do not wear a ribbon in my braid—I'm not five. But without the ribbon, the braid looked more like a weird growth sprouting from the side of my face, and I did not want another pig straw on my hands.

"You look like one of those Fisher-Price people," Jack teased.

"Whatever . . ." But he was sort of right: we all looked a bit like wooden peg toys with round plastic faces. Except Archie.

"Okay, so you've got the people. Now you need words. What do you guys usually talk about?" This again? We talked about everything. Okay, not true. We didn't talk about bedpans, tissues, ice water, or her father.

"Ooh, I know. Presidents, YouTube, and . . ." Could I really not name three things we talked about?

"Presidents? Like current events?" asks Jack.

"No, the dead ones, mostly."

"You guys sound like fun to hang out with."

"You and I talk about fish and doughnuts,

which makes us sound pretty boring—and pretty weird, too!"

"And we are not boring!" he announced. He surveyed the room, looking for inspiration. "Okay, let's think. . . . What does she . . . like to . . . eat?"

"Easy—french fries! But I don't think we've ever had a conversation about french fries."

"Okay, if you couldn't talk, what three words would you need the most?" Whoa, Jack was really taking this seriously.

"That's an impossible question."

"Let me see one of those things again," he said, gesturing toward the stack of charts Monica had given us. He grabbed one randomly:

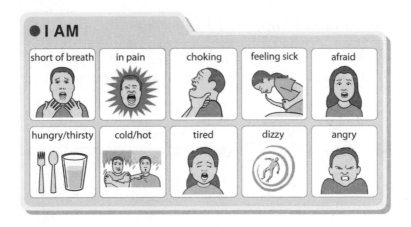

"Try this," he said. "Don't say anything for a minute. But write down three things that pop into your head that begin with 'I am' or 'I want.'"

Huh? Weird. But I ripped out a piece of paper from the sketchbook for Jack and then we sat in silence. After one minute, I had:

I am hungry.

I want to go running.

I want to meet your brother.

Jack glanced at my list and stood quickly, tossing his own list onto the table as he walked away. "I gotta go. I forgot about something I have to do." He always seemed to arrive—and depart—in a hurry. I read his list:

I want a cheeseburger.

I am a feminist. ☺

I want things to be different.

I compared the two lists—*I am, I want.* Looks like Jack and I were both pretty self-centered—or can you help but sound that way when your sentences have to start with *I am* or *I want*? Was Riley having the same kinds of *I am, I want* thoughts?

I am scared.

I want to go home.

I want to get better.

Or maybe just, *I want to tell everyone whose fault this really is.*

No way was I drawing *that*.

It was my fault—100 percent my fault.

On that night before Coney Island, before the Cyclone, before *everything*, when I got back from my very last run before all this, Riley had let me borrow her phone to text with Marisol.

I wrote: CYCLONE COUNTDOWN!

Mari: RU NERVOUS?

Me: YAAASSSSS!

Mari: TEXT ME WHEN IT'S OVER!!

I had just texted a thumbs-up back to her, when the phone rang. This came up:

 GEORGINA

I had the phone in my hand, so I answered it. "Hello?"

"Hi, beautiful!" a man's voice said.

"Uhhhh . . . ," I'd said. *Beautiful?* I'd thought.

"Riley?" His voice was deep. Like, not a thirteen-year-old-boy deep. And not even a fifteen-year-old deep. And definitely not like girl-friend-from-school deep.

"Um, no." I'd pulled the phone away from my ear to double-check the screen name, and by the time I was back listening, the Beautiful Guy had hung up. And Riley was lunging at me for her phone.

I held it away from her. "Who was that?"

"Nobody. It's nobody," she said in a voice that sure didn't sound like it was nobody. "Give me my damn phone." She grabbed for it again. I held it farther away. "Give. It. To. Me!" she said, her voice getting sharper. And sounding nervous.

And then I got it.

"Are you kidding? You have a boyfriend! He—he sounds like he's twenty-one!" I said. I stared at her. "What is wrong with you?"

"No, I absolutely do not! Give me my phone!" She lunged for it again, and now we both had our hands around it. My mind was racing. Riley had a boyfriend who called her beautiful, who was a *man*. That was so . . . so . . . wrong. And it was stupid! And, and . . . dangerous! We even had *classes* about this!!

"I'm calling him back right now and telling him how old you are!"

"Nora!! I swear, I'm gonna kill you. Just shut up!" I'd never seen her so mad.

"You didn't meet him on the Internet, did you?" I asked, still gaping.

"No!" Now she was yelling. "Just give me the freakin' phone!"

"What's going on up there, girls?" Aunt Mo shouted from the bottom of the stairs.

"Nothing, Mom!" said Riley, her voice suddenly sweet and easy.

"I can't even believe you!" I said, keeping my voice as low as I could without sounding like I was backing down. Archie growled at me.

"Just leave it alone," Riley was saying. "You have no idea what you're talking about."

Now I was glaring. "So why did you give him a fake name in your phone? Why would you do that if you weren't trying to hide him? I'm not an idiot!" My heart was pounding. Riley'd never done anything so stupid before. So, so stupid.

"You don't understand," she said, tugging again at the phone. "You're too young to understand, Nora. Just drop it!"

"Drop it?" I said. "How can I drop it? I already

know. You could get hurt. You could . . . you could disappear! It happens all the time!"

"It does not happen *all the time.*"

The phone lit up in our hands.

 GEORGINA

"Just give me the phone," Riley said, suddenly, oddly calm. "I'm sorry I yelled. I just got freaked out."

I had no idea what I was supposed to do. Riley pulled back hard on the phone, but I did too, pulling us even closer together. Then she did something I never thought she would do: she hit me. She took one hand off the phone and hit me square in the shoulder and knocked me off my feet. I fell back and hit the dresser so hard it tipped and almost everything on it—a lamp, her jewelry box, a makeup tray—crashed to the floor. Archie went wild, jumping between us. He towered over me, barking at me, baring his teeth.

Aunt Maureen came bounding up the stairs. "Is everybody okay?"

Riley was breathing hard but held out her hand to help me. I didn't take it. Archie was now standing guard halfway between Riley and me.

"*What* is going on up here?" Aunt Mo demanded suspiciously, eyeing the stuff all over the floor.

"Nothing, Mom," Riley said quickly. "We were goofing around. We just fell. Over the dog. I tripped over Archie." Her hand was still out to me. I still ignored it. "Nora got tangled up in my feet. . . ."

Aunt Maureen narrowed her eyes as if she didn't quite believe her, but nodded. "Time to cool off—and relax. Okay, guys?"

The phone lay facedown between us, six inches from Aunt Maureen's feet. Archie hadn't relaxed a muscle; he looked ready to go for my jugular.

The phone rang once more, and this time I literally jumped. Startled, Archie lunged at me, his teeth inches from my face. I kicked at him to protect myself.

"NO!" Aunt Maureen shouted, Archie yelping as she violently yanked him back. "DOWN!" Aunt Maureen was in *his* face now.

The phone was still ringing. Riley reached over,

but Aunt Maureen was quicker. As she picked the phone up, I could see the screen. I swallowed hard and stared at Riley, but she was staring at her mother, wide-eyed with panic.

 GEORGINA

Please answer it. Please answer it. Did I want her to answer it???

"You broke your phone?" Aunt Maureen cried out. She turned the front of the phone outward, furious. A crack zigzagged from the top of the screen to the bottom.

 GEORGINA

"I'm sorry, Mom—" Riley gulped.

 GEORGINA

Please answer it. I wanted someone else to know. *Please.*

"This is the *second* one you've broken! I am *not* getting you a new one.

 GEORGINA

"You're just going to have to save up until you

can fix it yourself," Aunt Mo went on, thrusting the phone back at Riley.

 GEORGINA

I locked eyes with my cousin. She had gone completely white. Her hand holding the phone was shaking.

Don't answer it.

It stopped mid-ring.

Aunt Maureen was not done with Archie, either. "Bad dog!" she told him. He looked at Riley for help, but all she cared about was the phone. "He wouldn't have hurt you, honey," Aunt Maureen said to me. "I promise."

"I know," I said, not believing her, but wanting her to feel okay enough to *leave.*

My aunt took Archie by the collar and led him away like a prisoner. Once they disappeared down the stairs, I picked myself up.

"Listen, I swear to you, I'm not doing anything stupid," Riley whispered when her mother was out of earshot. "I'm not sneaking out to see anyone. I gave him a fake phone name so I could have some privacy. That's all. My mom doesn't like when I talk to boys, but I'm almost *fourteen!*" *Privacy.* All of a sudden she needed privacy.

"Whatever," I said. What dawned on me in that last long minute was that when the dog went for me, Riley had gone for the phone. "You know what? You can have all the stupid boyfriends you want."

"He's not my boyfriend! I swear! Nora, promise me. Promise you won't tell. . . ."

"Do what you want." If she didn't care that her dog tried to bite me in the face, I wasn't going to care what she did either.

"I pinkie promise you *on my father's grave,* it's not like that. It's just a friend of a friend. It's nothing."

"What?" I gasped. "Is your father dead?"

"He is to me," she said. She plopped down on her bed and piled her hair up on her head, cinching it with a band. I was tired of her surprises— and her drama. I was seeing her in a different way in that moment—and not a good one.

"Fine, whatever," I said. "Nice code name."

"It's not a *code* name. It's just that, you know my mom; she'll get the wrong idea and then she'll totally freak out and take away my phone. You know she will."

Riley was right about that. If she was talking to a man on the phone, Aunt Maureen wouldn't just take the phone away, she might smash it to pieces, and Riley would be grounded until college.

"I'm sorry about the dog." So she *did* know. "The fight just scared him, that's all." *Scared me, too,* I wanted to say. But now I wanted this fight to be over, so I got over it.

"Who is he, anyway?" I asked, finally making eye contact with her.

"He's just someone from school," she said, holding my gaze. "He sounds older than he is."

"Promise?"

"I promise," she said, stepping closer to me. "And you have to promise me you won't tell."

"I already did."

"Promise again."

"I promise."

And I felt so awful making that promise that I wasn't torn anymore. I really wished Aunt Maureen had answered that phone.

So here it is in a nutshell: A phone, a fight, the dog.

I don't know how to draw *a promise*. But that's okay, because as it turns out, I don't know how to keep one either. Did I break the promise? Technically . . . no. But I *used* it to my tactical advantage. I *abused* it, stomped on it, destroyed it, and ran it over and left it for dead. Let's just call it "broken" because it sure as heck wasn't in one piece anymore.

So, here's the truth about what happened right before Riley and I got on the Cyclone in Coney Island—a truth I can't seem to tell if Riley remembers. Riley had been twelve steps behind me at the Cyclone when I broke that promise. And breaking that promise (in less than twenty-four hours, that's how horrible a cousin I am!) led to everything that happened next. On the way up the ramp to the roller coaster, Riley had let go of my hand. "I can't do it," she'd cried, turning around and walking away. "I'm sorry. I'm really sorry. I can't!"

What? She couldn't ditch me now! We were so close! "You have to!" I had cried out. "Please! I can't go by myself!" I stomped my foot like a little kid. I grabbed ahold of her shirt. It was covered in sweat, so I let go fast and ran to stand in front of her.

"I'm sorry, Nora. I'm too scared." Tears had sprung to her eyes. "You don't need me. You'll be fine. I'll wave to you from the ground. I can take your picture, for your essay!" She shoved me to the side to walk by me.

"I do so need you!" I called after her. "You *prom-ised* you would come with me, and you have to!" Riley kept walking. The line for the roller coaster continued to build. I was running out of time.

"Riley!" Now she wouldn't even turn around. "Fine!" I screeched. "If you break your promise to me, then I will break my promise to you!" I had to cross my arms over my chest to calm myself.

She whirled around. "What promise?"

Riley was blocking most of the line now, glaring at me with her hands on her hips. People started squeezing past us to get to the roller coaster, muttering under their breath, clearly annoyed. Riley didn't care. No surprise. *Please,* I had thought, *please don't. I don't really want to break this promise.* "What promise?" she demanded.

I didn't want to break it. I really didn't. Or did I? The other part of me from last night, torn again, wanted her to keep walking so I could tell Aunt Mo. So I had a *reason* to tell her. She kept walking. Then I knew. I wasn't torn.

"Georgina!"

Riley froze.

"Georgina!" I yelled again, even louder.

I was getting on that roller coaster.

So was she.

My chest was tight and my hands were in fists at my side. I was scared either way. Scared she would walk away from me and scared she would come toward me. If she walked away, would I actually tell her mother about her boyfriend? Wasn't that the right thing to do anyway? Riley was staring daggers at me, but at least she turned around. I guess choosing between walking toward me or walking away from me depended on which thing scared *her* more—the shakiest, oldest Abraham Lincoln roller coaster in the world or her mother finding out the truth about *Georgina*.

Well, now we all know the answer to that one.

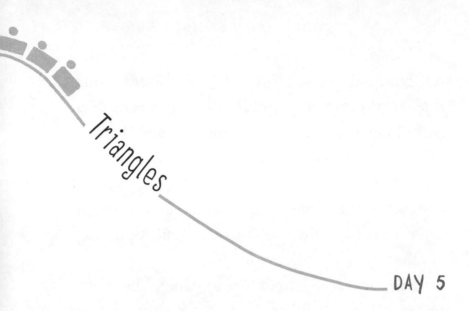

The next morning was off to a bad start before we even stepped foot in the hospital. The parking was so bad that after half an hour, Dad gave up and dropped us off so he could continue driving around the neighborhood. I knew it was about to get worse as soon as the elevator doors opened on the PICU. It was just a flash at first, that something, somehow, was different. The normal buzz of the PICU was there . . . but off a beat. A nurse in rocket-ship scrubs looked up at us from a computer at the nurses' station for a moment and quickly glanced away. I exchanged a tense look with my mother as something seemed to register with her, too, because then she sprinted down the hall at

144

her ER speed. I was right behind her and barely past the first two rooms in the hall when I realized what was different. Riley's cube—normally a constant hive of activity—was dark. That was the beat, the difference. A pattern of light you don't know you're expecting, until it changes. I flashed back to Monica's warning, *Be prepared for uncertainty.*

Mom and I stood confused in the middle of an empty cube. No Riley. No bed. No Aunt Maureen. The computer monitors were dark. The black oxygen ball lay flat in its outlet. I stared at my mother, terrified, and watched the color drain out of her face. "What's happened? Where's Riley?" Her voice cracked. An orderly walked by, pushing a patient in a wheelchair. "Please, where is Riley? Is she okay?" *Please. Please. Please.*

"I'm sorry," he answered, rolling right past us and shrugging. I felt my own heart pumping faster. Everything had been good last night! How fast could things change? *The speed of a roller coaster,* I reminded myself.

My mother pulled us into the hallway. "Nora, just wait here." She parked me beside the door to the women's restroom, the same way she had parked me outside the emergency room curtain almost a week earlier. "Let me get some . . . information. Stay . . . right . . . here."

"I want to come with you!" But she was gone already, heading to the nurses' station. I closed my eyes and held my breath, trying to imagine the oxygen traveling through my bloodstream and wondering what my P-SOCKS reading would be. Riley's quiet, empty room had left me dizzy. No words, no questions, no grunting, no parents, no small talk, no wolves. I was scared out of my mind. Rocket-ship-scrub nurse looked up when my mother reached her.

"Please, I'm looking for my niece. She's been here for days and now she's not and I don't—"

"PEDIATRIC CODE BLUE, SEVEN SOUTH. PEDIATRIC CODE BLUE." The announcement was broadcast to the entire floor.

Code Blue?

Every available person on the floor seemed to run past us, heading toward the end of the hall-way. Doctors and nurses streamed into the cube at the end of the hall, including the nurse in rocket-ship scrubs, her swivel chair still spinning at the nurses' station, she had jumped up so fast.

"PEDIATRIC ICU CODE BLUE. SEVEN SOUTH. PEDIATRIC ICU CODE BLUE."

A nurse escorted a sobbing woman out of the Code Blue room, an arm draped over her shoulder. I stood gaping at her. *The mother? Moved out of the room for her own good?* Mom gently turned me to face the other way, toward the elevator. Then I had a horrifying thought. I snapped my head back. Is that Colin's room? *Where the hell was his room?* Frozen, here I go, felt it. Always my legs first. Instincts are supposed to be fight or flight, right? I always got stuck somewhere right in between.

"Come on," my mother urged, back to being frantic about Riley, pulling me away. "Let's . . . go." I searched for Jack in the crowd, but there was so much movement and so many people—running in and out—that it was impossible. Dr. Mejia arrived, people cleared the way.

My mother was still pulling me. "Come on."

Worried faces emerged from the other cubes but quickly retreated. *Too personal. Too private. Too close.*

"Paige! What are you doing up here?" An oddly familiar voice from the elevator end of the hall-way. "I've been looking everywhere for you!"

"Oh no, not now," groaned my mother. "I can't do this now. . . ." In the middle of the deserted end of the hallway was my aunt Elayne, all the way from California.

Aunt Elayne was all smiles as she strode toward us. "Maureen has been trying to text you."

"Text me? Why?" asked Mom, her voice tinged with panic. "Where is she?"

"Hello, Nora." Aunt Elayne gave me a peck on the cheek. "It's good to see you." I stared at her like she had just dropped out of the sky. When did she get here?

"Maureen's on another floor with Riley," Aunt Elayne offered nonchalantly. "Or at least, that's where she told me she was, but I can't find her."

"What?" My mother looked visibly annoyed. "What floor? What are you talking about, Elayne?" I thought Mom was going to shake her.

Some of the staff who had responded to the Code Blue began to empty out of the Code Blue room.[31] Some paired off and left the floor, a few huddled outside the cube, the shades now drawn. The door of the cube closed. Code Blue over. But . . . good over? Or bad over?

"Is Riley okay, do you know?" I asked my aunt Elayne the question that never gets a straight answer.

"Of course," she answered, without giving it much thought. "Why wouldn't she be?"

"Where *is* she?" my mother demanded, this time inches from her sister's face. Aunt Elayne pulled away.

"She's on the pediatric floor."[32] Again, cool and casual, like Riley was exactly where we should expect her to be. "Mo said her cardiologist[33] cleared her. I swear, it's been a game of cat and mouse since I got here! I came up here, nobody. I tracked her down to the eighth floor, but nobody was in the room. I texted you three times. . . ."

---

[31] Not all hospitals use the same "code" designation, but they all have a code that lets the staff know that someone is having an emergency, usually cardiac arrest—their heart has stopped.

[32] The floor or section of the hospital that treats kids—usually from about three years old and up. They can be very sick but don't require quite the monitoring of the ICU.

[33] Reminder: heart doctor.

My head was spinning. I just wanted to sit down. Right there on floor.

"Riley's been moved off the floor." It was Audra, one of our favorite nurses, sounding more tense than usual. "I tried to find her new room number, but it's not in the system yet."

"What is she doing in pediatrics?" Mom was fumbling with her phone, which I could see was lit up with texts and messages. "Mike, Riley's out of PICU. . . . I know! Eighth floor . . . I'll meet you there. . . ." Aunt Elayne threw up her hands in disgust.

"I am *not* getting back in the elevator again!" Aunt Elayne announced to nobody.

"I'll be right back," I said, but my aunt was now on the phone too.

I did a quick lap around the PICU, trying to look casually and quickly for Jack in every cube. Nothing. I poked my head into the family room. No Jack. Could I have missed him? My heart started pounding. Could he be behind the shade in the Code Blue room right now? I immediately abandoned a bad decision to just plant myself in the hallway to see who came out of the Code Blue room. I didn't want to see Jack if he was coming out of there; I only wanted to make sure he wasn't *in* there. What was I going to say if I bumped into him? *There was a Code Blue! You have to go check on your brother!*

I doubled back in the opposite direction, this time picking up my pace at the Code Blue room and then again at Riley's empty room. Two quiet rooms, two very different outcomes. But for who?

I found the staircase and pulled on the door, momentarily panicked that I might set off an alarm. I didn't. The stairwell was empty. I jogged down the two flights of steps to pediatrics, but then I turned and went back up to the PICU: two flights up, two flights down, two flights up. I didn't know where I wanted to go. I was dizzy and sweating. Finally I threw my weight against the cold horizontal bar of the door back on the tenth floor, my sweat suddenly cold, my legs shaky. There I spotted Jack chatting casually with Monica outside her office. He waved—an everyday Code Regular wave. And then my anxiety and my adrenaline plummeted. I forced the bathroom door open with my hip, hands over my mouth. Into the first open stall, before I could get to my knees, I vomited, until my stomach was empty, until my legs stopped shaking. Then I sat on the floor until I could catch my breath.

In the stall next to me, the door swung open and quickly closed. Rocket-ship scrubs. Then the sound of crying.

Code Blue: bad over.

The pediatrics hallway was not quite the sunny yellow of the PICU, but the optimistic decor was present in the cloud-and-sky theme all around the top border. The high-tech control-center patient cubes were gone too. Each room had a small window to the hallway, and though some rooms had only one patient in them, others had two. The cheerful scrubs were still here too.

"Riley McMorrow?" I asked at the nurses' station.

"Eight-A," answered a nurse, without looking up from a chart. "I just checked her in!"

"Why isn't she in a private room?" Aunt Elayne was asking my father as I walked in. They were facing each other, sitting on opposite sides of Riley.

The curtain dividing the room was half-open, revealing an empty, unmade bed and a chair covered in random belongings: a sweatshirt, a drugstore bag, and a stuffed giraffe.

"Hey, Dad." I had splashed my face with water and hoped I looked reasonably normal. Well, at least for here.

"Hi, sweetheart." He furrowed his brows. "You okay?"

"Took the stairs," I answered. "Just winded. Where's Mom?" It occurred to me that maybe only two visitors were allowed in pediatrics—and Mom might have used the rule to duck out. Maybe I could too?

"With Aunt Maureen and—"

"I think a private room would be better," interrupted Aunt Elayne, "for everyone."

"I'm not sure Maureen is worried about that," answered my dad politely. He didn't put down the *Patient Rights: A Guide for Patients, Caregivers, and Families* pamphlet he was reading.[34]

---

[34] What are your rights? you might ask. Well, they include the right to receive treatment without discrimination as to race, color, religion, sex, national origin, disability, sexual orientation, source of payment, or age.

"She would have privacy, for one thing." Aunt Elayne just kept going. "Don't you think Riley would like some *privacy?*" *Privacy for Riley?* My aunt had a lot to learn. Privacy in her room? No. Her phone? Yes.

"I don't know," my father said with a sigh. He put the pamphlet down. "Riley, would you like some privacy?" I couldn't tell if he was being sarcastic or just asking. I don't think my aunt could either.

Elayne ran her hands through her hair. "I thought she was asleep."

Riley was not sleeping. Her eyes were half-closed, and she was still, but she definitely wasn't asleep. Her HR dropped when she was asleep, I knew. She was a solid and steady seventy-eight—a very-much-awake heart rate.

Elayne stood up, still not addressing Riley. "Why isn't Maureen here? Shouldn't she be here?" Frenetic energy practically bounced off the walls. I wished she would sit down.

"She's with Monica, the child life specialist," Dad answered, turning back to the *Patient Rights*.

"What the hell is a child life specialist?"

"A social worker, Elayne." Dad said this like

he had known what a child life specialist was his whole life, in a tone that sounded very much like a grown-up *duh*.

"A social worker?[35] Why does Riley need a social worker? Is she on drugs? Is that how this happened? You know where she got that from, don't you?" What did that mean? I shot Riley a look out of pure habit. Her eyes weren't half-closed anymore. They were laser-focused on Elayne, who still hadn't even acknowledged her. My aunt barreled on without waiting for any answers. "How does this kind of thing happen? This doesn't feel possible."

"There was a problem—with her heart." Dad was using his trying-to-be-patient voice.

"Do you trust the doctors here?" Aunt Elayne asked next.

"What does that even mean?" My mom entered the room just in time to hear the question, and her irritation was immediate. "Honestly, Elayne, you've been here all of ten minutes. Why don't

---

[35] Social workers help people solve and cope with problems in their everyday lives. Sometimes when people are struggling with big problems—like drugs or depression or chronic illness—social workers help them find additional resources, too. You may even have one who works in your school.

you take a breath before you start spouting opinions about things you don't understand?"

Aunt Elayne didn't flinch; it was as if they had always carried on conversations this way. "Well, Brooklyn isn't exactly known for its medical care, is it?"

My mother was speechless. For three seconds. "I'm not sure how we made it through the last week without guidance, Elayne. Maybe if you'd been around more when Mom was sick, it might have turned out better."

Aunt Elayne finally flinched.

Dad finally closed the pamphlet and stood slowly. "Paige, maybe—"

"Mom has nothing to do with this! And if it were *your* daughter," continued Aunt Elayne, "wouldn't you want her to be in a hospital in Manhattan instead of in a place famous for its hot dogs, or cheesecake, or whatever?" She walked toward my mother, the better to get in her face.

Dad moved quickly over to them. "Nora, honey, please. Step outside."

My mom was livid. "Elayne's the one who should step outside!" *Whoa.*

Over Mom's shoulder, I caught sight of Aunt Mo in the hallway. I don't know what it looked like from out there, but she practically sprinted through the door.

"Elayne!" cried my aunt Maureen, arms outstretched. "You found us! I'm so glad you're here!" They bear-hugged at the end of the bed for a very long time.

Mom left the room without another word and Dad followed. I stared after them, not sure what to do, when I felt a hand on my arm. Riley's fingers were closing tightly around my wrist. She caught me completely off guard, and I jerked my arm free.

Riley's heart rate jumped from 78 to 92.

I declined my parents' invitation to take a walk. I knew my mother was going to vent about Aunt Elayne, and I didn't really need to hear about it.

"Riley called it the Sullivan Triangle." I was explaining the crazy dynamic between my mom and Aunt Elayne to Jack up in the PICU family room. I felt funny being there because Riley wasn't in intensive care anymore, but I knew that's where I would find Jack.

"Doesn't really matter who they are," Jack said reasonably. "There's three of them—your mom and your two aunts. Triangles don't work. That's why you and I get along. If there were another kid in here, two of us would be more similar than the third one. Always works that way. If the other kid was a girl, then I would probably be the 'out.' Or if the other kid was a boy, then you would be the 'out.' One person is always a little bit left out when there are three."

"But Elayne is the outsider," I argued. "She lives in California and she just showed up now! Like practically a week later! Then, all of a sudden, Aunt Mo walks into the room and my *mom* is the outsider!"

"Depends on the situation," he said. "It's a *fluid* triangle. Depends on what's going on *around the triangle*. You know?"

I nodded, even though I wasn't so sure I got it. Jack could tell, though, because he kept right on explaining. "Name any three people and I'll tell you who the outsider would be."

"Me, you, and Riley," I said.

"FLUID!" he answered. "You guys are cousins,

so I might be the outsider. But you and I are, well, healthy, and Riley is not." I cringed. "At least, not right now. So in that case, *she* could be the outsider."

"Same for me, you, and Colin, I suppose."

"Yeah." He shifted uncomfortably. "Pick something else."

"Me, you, and P-SOCKS," I said. "But you can't make him the outsider because he's a fish! That's too easy!"

"Can you swim?" he asked.

"Yeah, of course."

"There it is. I can't swim. I'm the outsider." Huh. I thought everybody learned how to swim. I tried again. "Fine. Make me the outsider." I thought it was a good challenge. It wasn't.

"You are technically out of the intensive care, and P-SOCKS and I aren't going anywhere." A lump filled my throat so fast I almost choked on it. I didn't know what to say. "See how the fluid triangle works?" Jack went on.

"Yeah, I get it," I said, and I did, but I also got something else. I got that Riley was going to be released from the hospital someday and Colin probably wasn't going home. "I'm sorry, Jack. That was a bad example."

"It's okay," he nice-lied. He stretched out his legs. They practically touched the fish tank. He waited for more triangle examples, but I didn't offer. The silly way I thought about triangles was different from the way Jack did—and I was worried about leading the conversation somewhere I didn't want to go.

"I should probably head back." I gathered up my stuff, avoiding eye contact with Jack as he watched me. "I'm meeting my dad for lunch. We're going out today, for a change."

"Okeydoke." He wasn't looking at me anymore.

"Need anything?" Food. My go-to for awkward moments.

"Plenty," he answered, but he was looking at the fish.

DAY 5 ½

Riley had a roommate—the owner of the stuffed giraffe, I presumed. I hadn't seen her yet; the curtain that divided the room in half had been closed most of the day. But I had heard her, plenty. We all had. Her name was Jennifer, and she must have called every single person she knew and told them that she had had a terrible accident and fallen down the steps. "And it was like messed up so bad that I had to have surgery to fix it, and now I have a rod in my foot. For real . . ." Jennifer told her story over and over and over again in excruciating detail.

Aunt Elayne made sure my mother wasn't looking and then used the board:

I stifled a giggle. But she wasn't done. She went to:

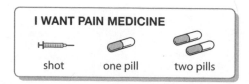

My giggle got away from me and Aunt Elayne winked. Mom looked up for just a moment and then went back to the pile of work she had begun to bring with her to the hospital. Today was the first day she seemed fully involved in it, and I'm pretty sure Aunt Elayne had something to do with that. Dad's work was piling up too, and after Mom promised to "remain calm," he opted to do his work in the family room.

Riley could actually sleep despite Jennifer's constant babble. As Jennifer repeated the story for the umpteenth time, I closed my eyes and pictured it happening. Jennifer at the top of the stairs. Jennifer's bright orange flip-flops. The bottom of the left flip folding under on the top step. Jennifer flying forward! Jennifer grabbing for the banister, but missing!

The tumble! The yelling! A heap at the bottom of the staircase. The crying! I knew it was wrong, but the sketchbook was already open in my lap. I really had to dig for an orange pencil, but I found one.

As Jennifer finished her 1,011th phone call with an "OMG, I might totally need a cane!" Aunt Elayne had reached her limit. She went to the curtain. "Could you please keep it down? My niece is trying to sleep!" Jennifer did not appreciate the scolding and made another phone call almost *immediately*.

"Hey, it's me. I'm in the hospital. . . ."

"Jesus! Nobody gives a sh—" Mom pulled Aunt Elayne away from the curtain, smiling even though I don't think she wanted to. They tripped over each other and both started to laugh. That's when I held up my drawing:

There was a very, very long and uncomfortable pause as they both stared at it.

"That is . . . terrible!" My mother was not amused.

But Aunt Elayne burst out laughing. "That is *brilliant*! Let's make a plane out of it and fly it over the curtain!" Mom actually laughed as she tried to object, and couldn't stop. I had never seen my mother laugh that hard. Her face went beet red! People were looking in the window now, smiling at us as they walked by. *Look at the happy people, making the best of a bad situation.* Nope, just some really bad people making fun of someone else's bad situation.

"O," said Riley. I shifted in my seat, worried that Riley was having that same feeling you get when you walk into a room and everyone suddenly stops laughing. "O" was a word, for sure. It wasn't "hello," but that's what she meant by it. I *understood* her!

"Show her," prodded Aunt Elayne. She had calmed down—somewhat—and reached across the bed to turn the book toward Riley herself.

I waited anxiously for Riley's reaction. Her

good hand drifted to the picture and she ran her fingers over it. She looked confused, but we really couldn't explain because, well, the butt of our joke was lying five feet away in a hospital bed. Riley's cheeks twitched. A smile? A grimace? A muscle spasm?

"Hey, it's me . . . I fell down the steps!" Jennifer, as if in on the joke, launched into yet another phone call. Aunt Elayne doubled over again and plopped herself on my mother's lap.

The first time we had laughed in days—and I mean guffawed—was at the expense of someone who had tripped down an entire flight of steps and was recovering from surgery. Clearly, we were not good people.

"What else you got?" asked Aunt Elayne, getting a hold of herself, pointing toward the sketch pad. It was Riley who pushed the book toward me. Mom encouraged Aunt Elayne off her lap with a little shove. Riley's eyes now settled on each one of us at her bedside, a few seconds on Mom, a few on Aunt Elayne's red face, runny with mascara, and then a few seconds on me.

"C'mon, Nora, don't hold back," said Aunt

Elayne. "I've seen you scribbling in that book. Have you got any other good drawings for us?"

"Um, well," I stumbled, "I made this." I pulled out the Fisher-Price drawings I had done with Jack:

Riley

~~Maureen~~
~~Mom~~
Moo-Moo

Uncle Mike

Aunt Paige

Archie

Nora

"That's cute," said Aunt Elayne, leaning over the end of the bed. Cute? Oh jeez. "Wait a minute! Where am I?"

"You weren't here yet," I answered.

"Hmmmph," from my mother. So much for laughing.

"Let me see that." Mom, looking at my Fisher-Price heads chart, nodding. "Do you recognize everybody, Riley?" Riley looked down at the notebook, but her eyes didn't move over the page.

"There's you, your mom, Archie!" Riley suddenly reached for it.

"Moo-Moo," she said quietly, her hand on the drawing of Aunt Maureen. "Moo-Moo." Her heart rate went up—seventy-two to eighty. She wanted her mother.

"She'll be back in a few minutes, honey," my mom reassured her. "She's meeting with Dr. Mejia." Elayne stepped away from the bed as my mom moved forward. Comfort was my mother's territory.

"O," Riley said again. It wasn't "hello" after all. It was the word you use when you have no idea what to say. The word you might use if you woke up in a room with your family laughing their heads off while you try to recover from a stroke and hope your mother is coming back soon. Even if she had a thousand words to choose from—and she didn't—what else could you say to that?

Our rides home at night were traditionally pretty quiet. My parents were exhausted, and more often than not, I slept. They weren't quiet tonight.

"I still can't believe Elayne," said my mother in the front seat. "I mean, why is she even here?

What's the point now? Tomorrow I'm going to ask her when she's leaving. I mean, does she really need to be here now, when things have calmed down? It's so *typical* of her!"

My dad sighed. "Well, maybe Maureen—"

"I mean, she's not even really here," my mother went on, working herself into a frenzy. "She's in a hotel half an hour away in the other direction. What exactly is the point?"

"Maybe she just wants to be here—"

"Is it helping Maureen? Isn't it enough that *we're* here? That Nora's here? I mean, Elayne is here now the same way she was here when Mom was dying. It's the same thing all over again. . . ."

Dad didn't answer, because it wasn't really a conversation. My mom was blowing off steam. Easier now because she had someone to be mad at. I wanted to defend Aunt Elayne and I wanted to tell my mother that I thought she was being a really good sister to Aunt Mo and I wanted to know more about what it was like when my grandmother died. But more than all those things put together, I really wanted Mom to finish her verbal assault on Aunt Elayne. I just couldn't do it—listening to people's anger is exhausting—I'd also had enough of trying to figure out what people really meant when they were talking. I did it with Riley every day, and it also felt an awful lot like the triangle conversation with Jack; every time I tried to play, it stopped feeling like a game.

DAY 6

It took an impossible two hours to get to the hospital the next morning because of an accident on the parkway that shut down all but one lane of traffic. This was another reason why Aunt Maureen stayed at the hospital, I finally understood. If she never left, she never had to worry about how or when she was going to get back. I had plenty of time to sketch in the backseat, which I did. I worked on a few Aunt Elaynes, which I didn't think my mother was going to appreciate— but she *was* here and she was on the team, whether my mother liked it or not. I finally settled on my third version and redid it onto the page with the rest of the family.

It was another eternity to park the car. The lot was full and we parked even farther away than we had in the rain two days ago—clear on the other side of the main road; we had to cross over six lanes of traffic to get to the hospital. It was a dangerous cross, too, even with the light, because cars were turning off the parkway. Seemed like cars were coming from every direction. It was hard to know where to look, so I held my father's hand, sketchbook tucked under my arm, and walked when he walked and stopped when he stopped.

When we finally made it to the eighth floor, Aunt Maureen was waiting for us outside Riley's door. She was beaming. "Ta-da!" she said, sweeping her arm out as if she were welcoming royalty into the room. There were too many of us—we would be over the visiting limit—but Aunt Mo insisted we all come into the room.

Whaaa? Then I saw.

Riley was sitting up in a chair!

My mother bent down to give Riley a hug. "Look at you!" Riley still had her tubes and wires and monitors, but there she was—in a chair! And I realized to my horror that I had never once, in all this time, pictured her any other place but the bed. Riley looked happy, if a little crooked, in the chair. I made a mental note to add a column of sparks.

"How long have you been sitting there?" teased my dad. "And where am I supposed to sit?" He gave her a hug after my mom's.

"Riley worked so hard this morning," explained Elayne, looking almost as happy as Aunt Maureen. "Jodi let her stay out of bed a few extra minutes just so you could see!" Despite staying in a hotel in downtown Manhattan, fourteen miles away, Elayne had beaten us to the hospital. We had missed the big reveal, but my aunt had been right on time.

"Jodi?" asked Dad. *Jeez, Dad, get a clue.* Even I knew who Jodi was.

"That's me. I'm Riley's physical therapist. Hi, everybody!" Riley had a physical therapist, an occupational therapist, a speech therapist, and even an art therapist.[36] Jodi was standing in front of Riley now, adjusting some kind of belt around

---

[36] The road to medical abbreviations is tricky! Occupational therapists are often referred to as OTs and physical therapists as PTs, but speech therapists are not referred to as STs, nor are art therapists referred to as ATs.

her. It was a few inches wide and wrapped around Riley's waist, pinching her gown. This was the first time I had seen her physical therapy in action.

"She's going to do a lap around the hallway by the end of the week," Aunt Maureen announced. "Aren't you, sweetheart?"

Riley gave a thumbs-up sign with her good hand.

"We'll see," Jodi enthused. "We will be taking a few steps with a walker pretty soon. I like to get my patients up and out as soon as possible! For now, though, how about we get you back to bed?"

"No," teased Riley, with a small smile, looking as happy as I had ever seen her.

Jodi knelt in front of Riley on the floor and placed her hands on Riley's hips to help her scoot her body to the front of the chair. Then she moved Riley's feet farther apart on the floor. "Um . . . we're going to need a little more space here, guys. Could we thin out the crowd a bit?"

Neither Mom nor Aunt Elayne moved a muscle, so Dad bit the bullet and offered to stand in the hallway. "I'll step out. But I'm right here, so I can watch! I call the empty chair when I get back!"

Riley smiled a half smile at him. I think she liked that he was teasing her again.

"Any other volunteers?" Jodi insisted. When nobody moved, Aunt Maureen very clearly shot my mom a look. She stepped out.

"We're going to stand now," Jodi began. "Now remember, I'm going to help you with your weaker leg by placing my leg against your shin, right? Just like getting off the bed. On the count of three, you push off with your arms as much as you can, and don't worry, I'll have my arms around you. Ready? One, two, three . . ." Riley used her good arm to push herself up and leaned into Jodi for support. "Good job!" Jodi chirped. "Now straighten your legs and let's get you balanced." Riley was unsteady, and I could tell we were all holding our breath. Riley and Jodi stood like a couple doing a slow dance, even swaying a little. "We're going to turn now, Riley, so your back is toward the bed," Jodi now told her. "Remember how we practiced? Shuffle your feet as we turn, slowly, slowly." Riley was pivoting her body by shuffling her feet, the way you might do in a cramped space. "Great!" Jodi was grinning big-time. Riley was facing us now, standing mostly on her own, although Jodi still had her hands on her shoulders. "Now before you sit back on the bed, make sure you can feel the bed with the back of your legs so you know where you are." Riley nodded as she continued to shuffle a few inches backward, Jodi keeping her steady. Riley's face lit up when she felt the bed behind her, and she lowered herself down. We all exhaled when her butt made contact with the bed. I was actually sweating, and I wasn't doing anything. I couldn't believe how much work was involved in just moving three feet. Riley wasn't going to heal herself by resting anymore, like I had with the flu; she was going to heal by *working*—and working hard. Three feet at a time. One chair at a time. While I stared at her, I couldn't help but wonder if Jack was watching pieces of Colin fade away while I was watching pieces of Riley come back.

Riley needed help from Jodi to get her weak leg up onto the bed. When she was finally flat, she barely had the energy to pull the blanket over herself. Her breathing was heavy and she was beeping a little faster, but she didn't conk out. Instead she shuffled her communication boards around until she found what she wanted:

And I swear, we all screamed. Even Mom and Dad in the hallway! Yes, it was a quiet hospital scream, but Riley used the board! Spark! Spark! Spark! Spark spark spark spark!

"Good job!" Aunt Maureen was so excited, she filled Riley's cup to overflowing, and had to drink some off the top before handing it to Riley, who held the cup herself and sipped. Then she looked at me and pointed.

"No," said Riley, still pointing.

"I think . . . she means *Nora*," said Aunt Elayne, surprisingly.

"More drawings?" Aunt Maureen gestured to the notebook I was holding. Having just spent five minutes watching Riley struggle to stand up and sit down, I didn't feel like now was the right time to reveal what suddenly felt like a glorified arts and crafts project. *Look, everyone, I can draw monkeys and owls!* But Riley was looking at me expectantly, so I had no choice. I sat down on the chair that Riley had just been in. It was still warm.

Aunt Maureen reached for the book, slowly turning first one page, and then another.

Fries

NY Mets

Abe Lincoln

Summer

Tamarin Monkey

Owl

Singing

Dancing

Drawing

"Oh, Nora, is this for Riley? For her communication board?" Aunt Maureen blinked away tears.

"It's fantastic!" Then she held up a page. "Look, Elayne, you and the monkey have the same hair!"

"That was an accident!" I said quickly, hoping having monkey hair wasn't going to set Aunt Elayne off. "Besides, look, yours is curly and the monkey's is straight!" If she was mad, she didn't look it. I snuck a peek at Riley to see if I could read anything on her face. Nope. Nothing. Definitely no spark. None that I recognized, anyway.

"Are there more?" asked Aunt Maureen.

"I'm working on a few things," I said, pulling out a separate notebook where I practiced some of the pictures I wasn't so sure about. I showed them:

NYC   Taylor Swift

"I love it, sweetheart, thank you. Riley does,

too," Aunt Maureen said just as Dr. Mejia stuck her head in and motioned for my aunt to join her in the hall. The sketchbook was on the tray table in front of Riley now, but she wasn't looking at it.

"What is this, exactly?" asked Aunt Elayne. "I know, I know, I'm a little slow. . . ."

"Just Riley words, um, I mean words she might want to use." I had pointed at Riley, like she wasn't really there. Embarrassed, I looked back down at the french fries and the monkey. I wanted to string them all together and give them to Riley. *These are yours!*

Aunt Elayne turned to a page where I had carefully traced Riley's drawing:

Beside it I had left a blank box.

"What's the wolf for?" asked Aunt Elayne. "Is it for: 'Do you need anything?' Maybe an extra pillow . . . or a wolf?"

"Can you ask the nurse for an extra wolf?" she went on.

"I smell wolf. Check under the bed!" I realized that Aunt Elayne might be the funniest Sullivan sister.

"Walt." It was Riley. It didn't really sound like a real word, but it felt like Riley was trying to say something specific. I smiled at her, but it was a tomato-soup smile. *I'm pretending that you make sense, Riley. That I know what you mean.*

"What's the extra box for?" Aunt Elayne asked, either oblivious to the new sound or ignoring it.

"It's for Riley," I said. "In case she wants to add something."

"Oh," she said. There it was—the verbal cringe. She looked at Riley and then smiled at me with her own 100 percent tomato-soup smile. "Maybe when she's feeling a little better." She shifted around uncomfortably all of a sudden. "God, I hate hospitals."

"See." Riley. She put her good hand up to her face. Wait . . . See! "See" was a real word! Aunt Elayne stopped shuffling. We looked at each other, eyes wide, waiting for more.

"Sssseee," said Riley. "Ssseeee." She was leaning forward, trying to push herself up off the pillow. I think she was trying to get out of bed. I guess this was what agitated looked like.

"Do you want to see the pictures, honey? Do you want to point to something?" Aunt Elayne glanced at me. "Go get Maureen. She's better at this." I stuck my head into the hallway and spotted Aunt Maureen a few doors down. Dr. Mejia was gone and now Aunt Mo was talking to my parents. I motioned to them frantically. "Riley's trying to do something."

"See," Riley said softly, as her mother rushed into the room, my parents right behind her, no matter what the visiting rule was. She was sitting up as best she could, leaning back on her right arm for support. She was upset. She fell back down to the pillow and brought her hand to her face again.

"See what?" Aunt Maureen asked calmly, trying to follow Riley's eyes around the room to pinpoint what she was trying to say. "See? Aunt Elayne?"

My aunt Elayne suddenly gasped. "Oh my God, she can't see! Is she telling us she can't see! Has she gone blind?!!"

My mother made a move toward Aunt Elayne, but my dad pulled her back.

"So help me, Elayne . . . ," Aunt Maureen muttered. She held out her hand, letting us all know to keep back.

Riley shook her head again, this time very slowly, like she was losing patience. Her good hand was balled up in a tight fist. There was no doubt that she understood what everyone was saying. And it was very, very clear that she had something important to say.

"Can you see me?" *Really, Aunt Elayne???*

"See, see, see." Calmer now.

"Okay, okay, I think she's telling us she can see," said Elayne. "Thank goodness. Thank goodness. You can see, sweetheart. You can see!" I thought she was joking. She wasn't.

"She can see just fine!" Aunt Maureen snapped. Her first real flash of anger since this whole thing started. "She can see just fine and she can also understand you, so stop with the theatrics!"

"All right, I got it already!!" Elayne snapped back.

As their voices rose, Riley seemed to hone in

on them. She was looking from one to the other like she was watching a Ping-Pong tournament. So was I! It was nothing new to watch Mom and Aunt Elayne bicker. It was something else to see Aunt Maureen involved. And Aunt Mo clearly had a hyper Riley radar; she seemed to sense her daughter's surprise, because she turned from Elayne.

"You're okay, Riley. Mommy's here," cooed Aunt Maureen, switching back to her caretaker voice. The anger and frustration evaporated. *How did she do that?*

"See-e-e," Riley repeated. She turned her head, slowly, slowly on the pillow until she was looking straight at me. Then she very deliberately pointed at me.

"Are you saying 'she'?" said Aunt Mo. "Is that it, sweetheart? She who? She, Nora?"

"See," she said again, nodding, pointing. Aunt Mo tried to put a communication board in her hand, but Riley pushed it away.

"Maybe you should get some rest, honey," said Aunt Maureen, pulling the blanket up under Riley's chin. Riley laid her head back down on the pillow but kept her eyes on me. She closed them for a second. I thought she was going to sleep. Then she opened them suddenly and stared right at me. Her eyes flashed. She was telling me something. "See," she said. She pointed at me with her good hand.

And then I knew.

I knew exactly what she was trying to say, in front of everybody. She was trying to say, *See what you did to me.*

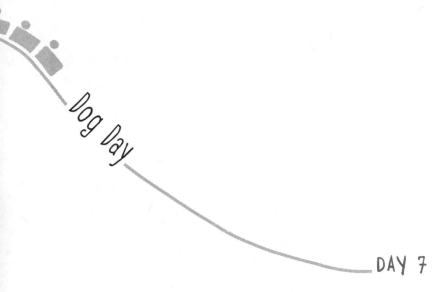

A rchie's breath was in my face. It was just about my least favorite way to wake up, but it was actually slightly better than the blare of Riley's alarm clock. I brushed my teeth, splashed water on my face, and went downstairs, Archie at my heels.

My parents were at the kitchen table, drinking coffee.

"Hi, honey." Mom had already set a place for me to eat breakfast. Froot Loops on the table.

The house was so quiet. "What time is it?" I asked.

"Almost ten thirty." Mom smiled—I think she might have actually slept late today too. I put the bowl on the table along with a banana. I was glad we were running late; that meant less time at the hospital. I know Riley's angry face. Riley had been angry when she pointed—something about those drawings had made her angry. Was it horrible to put singing and dancing and drawing? Three things she definitely could not do right now? Or was it the very simple fact that I was the reason she couldn't do any of those things?

"Sit down and eat, honey," said Dad. "No hospital today." I stiffened. No hospital?

"Why not?" I asked in alarm.

"Sit down, Nora." Mom looked so serious. "We thought it would be a good idea for you to take a break for a day." *Stay home?*

My stomach lurched. "Because Riley's mad at me?"

"What? No. Why would she be mad at you?" Mom put down her coffee cup.

"I don't know, she just seemed mad yesterday, that's all."

"Honey," said Dad, "I'm going to take the train back to Maryland today and you and your mom are going to stay here."

"What? You're going *home*?! That's not fair!" I

jumped out of my seat, slamming my palms on the table so hard the bowls jumped.

"I can't take any more time off, Nora," explained Dad. "I have to get back to work." He motioned for me to sit.

"Listen, honey," Mom began, "Riley *is* doing much better, but she still has a long way to go. . . . You and I . . . we . . . need to be here."

"Why?" As a punishment? To make me see what I had done? After Riley had glared and pointed at me, I had taken off for the family room again, this time to watch a baseball game in silence. I fell asleep in there too. It was really the only way to escape—fall asleep in the family room and people left you alone. Then I pretended to sleep in the car on the drive home and went straight upstairs after walking Archie. It's not that I blamed Riley for hating me; I didn't. It's just that I didn't have any defense. She was right   I *had* done this to her.

"We have to stay and help out, and Dad will be at work all day," Mom was explaining.

"He can go to work and I'll stay home," I pleaded. "I'm not helping here. You know it's true." I looked to my father for support, but he left the room, leaving

Mom to handle the argument.

"Honey, you can't stay home by yourself all day for the rest of the summer. And you *are* helping here, more than you know. It's important for Riley to have you here—she doesn't want to be surrounded by grown-ups and doctors and nurses all day. Trust me. And she's coming home soon; your aunt is going to need you even more."

Riley was coming home? "She's coming home?" I asked, shocked. "She can barely talk, Mom. Or walk! She's not better yet."

"Honey." She pushed her coffee cup away. After a moment, she said, "Nora, it's going to take more than a few weeks for Riley to recover."

"What do you mean?" Archie was at my feet, sniffing for fallen cereal. I shooed him off angrily. "Riley *is* getting better. She gets better every day. Even Dr. Mejia said she was getting strong, and she's practically walking!" I exaggerated. She was enough of her old self to pick a fight with me, I added, but only in my head.

"Sorry, Nora, but we're going to be here the rest of the summer. We're family. Everyone has to pitch in," Mom said in her end-of-discussion voice. She brought her cup to the dishwasher.

Wait. What? WHAT? Did she say the rest of the summer?

"The whole summer!" I cried out. Now I was desperate. "That's not fair!"

"I'm sorry, Nora." Mom closed the dishwasher.

"Mom, *please*?" I begged. "Just call Marisol. Her mom will let me stay with them. You *know* she will!"

Mom rubbed her eyes with the palms of her hands. Her well-rested look was gone. "I'm sure they would be happy to have you, Nora," she said. "Mari is a good friend and so is her mother, but the right place for you right now is exactly where you are."

I felt my options fizzling out. The whole rest of the summer? "It's so not fair! Why does *my* whole summer have to be ruined too?" I stormed out of the kitchen and up the stairs, and I didn't see the stupid Abraham Lincoln book on the floor and tripped over it. Dang it! Who knocked over my backpack? Everything was spilled on the floor! Archie!! I picked up the stupid book and threw it against the wall. Hard.

I kicked Abraham Lincoln again and he slid

across the floor and under the bed. I lunged for George Washington, pulled him off the shelf, and threw him to the floor. KICK. Calvin Coolidge. KICK! Ulysses S. Grant and his stupid horse! KICK. Franklin Delano Roosevelt, you too!! I pulled Andrew Jackson off the shelf and slammed him on the floor. KICK.

Nobody came running to see what the commotion was. Nobody yelled. After about twenty more kicks, I collapsed down on the bed. Archie whimpered and hopped up next to me. I'd looked at the disaster I'd created. Riley's books were scattered all over the floor. Her favorite books. Some were even ripped. I picked them up, flattened the pages, closed them carefully, and put them back. I'm sorry, George Washington. I'm sorry, Andrew Jackson. I'm sorry especially to you, Abraham Lincoln. I took Ol' Abe back off the shelf and slid the book back into my knapsack.

Archie moved closer to me, nudging my other hand with his giant face. I scratched the top of his head and he lowered it right against my leg.

"I'm sorry for everything, Archie," I confessed to the dog. "I'm really, really sorry." And that was the truth. Archie and I spent the rest of the day together on the couch staring at the television, then on the back deck staring at squirrels, and in the kitchen staring at each other as he waited for me to drop crumbs.

Walking

DAY 8

Y ou look like crap," Aunt Elayne declared before I was even all the way into Riley's room. She was right, of course. My mother sighed and ignored her, a classic move. No mention of my father, so I guess everyone except me had known that he was leaving yesterday. I hadn't even answered him when he had come to say good-bye before he left for the train station. He had kissed me anyway.

"Thanks," I muttered, flooding with relief when I saw Riley's empty bed.

"Rough night?" she asked. "Riley's gone to a PT session," she added. She studied me for a moment. "Maybe you should take a walk . . . or a nap . . . or . . . something."

"Not a bad idea," Mom agreed. "Why don't you head down to the family room? I'll meet you there in a bit."

"I meant a real walk, Paige; you know, with air and sunshine." Walking anywhere sounded good, actually. My legs were beginning to feel foreign to me from the hours I spent every day sitting in the car, sitting in the family room, sitting in Riley's room—and then sitting in a car again. My legs were getting depressed, and I didn't want it to spread to the rest of me.

"I don't think so," Mom replied.

"She needs to get fresh air every day," suggested my aunt, sounding surprisingly like a calm adult with a rational idea.

"Don't tell me what she needs," snapped Mom, now tapping away at her phone. "She's not your daughter." Oh no, not again. I wanted to tell both of them to shut up.

"I'll go with her," said Elayne. "How about that?"

Now I was quietly rooting for Aunt Elayne to win this one.

"Okay, Mom?" I added quickly. Honestly, I would have preferred to go alone, but it was better than nothing. Anything but being here when Riley got back. I studied my mother's face, not sure if she didn't want to let me go, or if she just didn't want to agree with her sister.

My mother sighed. "Fine, but only right outside the hospital." Mom was treating me like I was five years old. She hadn't mentioned the book-throwing incident during the drive this morning, but it was still pretty heavy on *my* mind. Was *I* losing it?

I could barely keep up with Aunt Elayne as she strode to the elevator. The doors opened and the elevator was packed, as usual. Aunt Elayne pushed right in and pulled me on with her. The fifteen strangers in the elevator car didn't faze her in the slightest—she kept right on talking like we were everybody's business. "What is wrong with your mother?" she was ranting. "What does she think I'm going to do with you? Throw you into traffic?"

The lady next to me hoisted her giant bag up on her shoulder, and it rubbed against my arm. I felt like it was some kind of protest for invading her space. It's not like I had a choice; there was no room to step aside.

"I don't know," I half mumbled, watching in surprise as Aunt Elayne stripped the cellophane off a pack of cigarettes she'd pulled from her bag and then put one in her mouth.

"You can't smoke in here!" the lady with the giant bag announced.

"Do I look like an idiot?" asked Aunt Elayne. The lady rolled her eyes.

"You smoke?" I literally did not know one single grown-up who smoked.

"Only on special occasions," she answered, the cigarette bobbing up and down at the corner of her mouth. The elevator door opened to a new crowd of people waiting to go up. "Come on. Let's go outside." She was three steps ahead of me already.

I pointed to the red sign on the building. NO SMOKING WITHIN 30 FEET.

"You've got to be kidding me. Fine. Come on. Ocean air will do us some good." She pulled a pair of sunglasses out of her bag and slid them on. "It's close, right? The beach?"

"Pretty close," I said, using a very loose definition of the word "close." I had never walked to it before, but Jack had said it wasn't too far.

We split up for a second to make our way around a group of people in front of the hospital. "This way," I said, nudging her to the left when we met up again. Aunt Elayne was moving more slowly now. Maybe she only rushed when she was trying to get away from my mother. I stopped at the corner to wait for the walk sign. Aunt Elayne rushed forward, but I pulled her back to the curb. She took the opportunity to light her cigarette, close her eyes, and take a long, long puff. When she exhaled, the smoke seemed to just hang there, trapped by the heat and humidity. "Which way?"

"Straight ahead," I said. Abraham Lincoln eyeballed me from a lamppost in front of a namesake high school across the six lanes of traffic.

"Are you sure?" She spun around in a little circle, trying to get her bearings.

"Positive." The beach was a straight shot from hospital, I knew that from the cab ride. The light changed at last and we crossed. I didn't blame Aunt Elayne for doubting me. There really was no reason to think that there was a beach nearby. At the next corner, we had the walk sign, but one after another, the cars made their turns right in front of us, like we weren't even there. Aunt Elayne let loose a string of obscenities, supplemented with hand gestures for those drivers with their windows closed. "Where the hell are we?" She wiped the sweat from her forehead with the back of her cigarette-free hand. She dug through her bag again, then handed me another pair of sunglasses.

"Just another few blocks, I think." I could see the raised subway tracks, so I knew the boardwalk wasn't much farther.

"If you say so," she said. "I'm just following your lead." But the closer we got to the beach, the more my throat tightened. At the next corner, Elayne flicked her cigarette into the street as she stepped off the curb, but I pulled her back.

"No, wait . . . ," I said. We were really far away from the hospital. It felt *too* far.

"What's the matter?" she asked.

"We should go back." I let go of her arm. "Mom will be worried."

"It's fine," she said, waving me off. "Here, I'll text her and let her know. She won't be happy about it, but she won't worry." She groped through her bag, looking for her phone. A dog shot out of a nearby apartment building and ran straight at us. Aunt Elayne pulled me out of the way. "Idiot," she grumbled, as the owner grabbed ahold of it.

"Really . . . let's go back," I insisted. The farther we got from the hospital, the more anxious I felt.

Aunt Elayne lifted her sunglasses to look at me. "What's wrong? Not that any of us are at our best, but you really do look terrible today, Nora. What is it?"

"I don't want to go for a walk," I lied. Well, not really. I just didn't really want to walk . . . there. But I didn't want to be at the hospital, either. There was just no place I actually *did* want to be. "I don't know how to explain it."

Now she lowered her sunglasses and looked at me over the frames. "Try."

"Riley's mad at me. I don't want to see her today." Even so, as soon as I said it, I wanted to take it back.

"Nora, honey, if I had to avoid people who were mad at me, I'd still be in San Francisco right now."

"Is that . . . what . . . what took you so long? To come?" There. It was out.

"I know . . ." She slipped her glasses to their regular position, covering her eyes. "I know I took my time getting here. I guess I was hoping that a few days would pass and I'd get a phone call saying . . . you know . . . that Riley would be just fine, some special treatment, a few weeks of therapy and she'd be back to her old self. But it didn't turn out that way." Aunt Elayne glanced away, choking back tears.

"Are you okay?"

"Yes, honey. I am. I'm just sad about all of it. All of this."

"Um, sad isn't okay," I said. "Sad is sad."

"Trust me," she said. "You can be sad and still be okay. And if you can't, you better learn." That was news to me. As we crossed the last street before the boardwalk, the smell of food was overwhelming. "Only in Brooklyn would the beach smell like onions." She pointed to the source—a huge restaurant sitting on the corner across Ocean Avenue. The split ramp up to the boardwalk was directly in front of us now. We stepped aside to make room for a family of bicyclists on their way down. They waved a thank-you and stopped in front of an ice-cream truck.

At the top of the ramp to the boardwalk, we could finally see the ocean. I could tell Aunt

Elayne was surprised. Wind whipped her hair into her eyes, and she held it back with one hand.

"I really need to sit down for a few minutes." Aunt Elayne put her arm around my shoulders. "Pretty close, my foot, by the way." She picked the first empty bench on the boardwalk, tugged off her shoes, and sat cross-legged. I did the same. The boardwalk was like a busy city sidewalk. People walked alone, in pairs, in groups; some gathered on either side and yelled to each other over the middle. Some cut across from one side to the other, headed down to the beach below. In front of it, the ocean hissed and pounded.

"Is that why you're not staying with us? Because of Mom?" I asked. A plump seagull with a limp seemed to be loitering in front of us, hoping for food.

Aunt Elayne swung her shoe in the seagull's direction. "I'm pretty comfortable where I am, and I'm out of everybody's way."

"Did you *ever* get along with my mother?"

She sighed. "I'm not here to fix my relationship with your mother; I'm here for Riley and for Maureen. I grab a taxi early in the morning and I get to spend a little extra time with Riley every day. Give your aunt Maureen a chance to take a shower and spend some time alone in the chapel." I didn't know that she was helping my aunt Maureen like that. I wondered if my mother knew?

"Are you going to stay until Riley's better?" Aunt Elayne was quiet for a minute, staring toward the water.

"Nora, Riley may not get much better. She may never be . . . the same as she was before." She was crying for real now, unable to hold back this time. I couldn't look at her. She hung her head, and it went on for a full minute or so. When she stopped, she wiped her eyes and said, "This is Riley now. This is the one I'm getting to know. In a strange way, I may be the lucky one. I didn't know the old Riley, not very well, so I'm not waiting for her to come back. You might want to think about that too." Now I choked back my tears. No! She was wrong! Riley was getting better every day. Aunt Maureen said it, my mother said it, even Dr. Mejia said it.

Riley had words.

She could sit in a chair.

She could eat with a spoon.

I could barely keep up with all the sparks!

"Shall we?" Aunt Elayne stood.

"Shall we . . . what?" I asked, confused.

"Walk down to the water," she said, picking up her shoes. "Why come all the way to the beach and not actually go into the water? Well, our feet, at any rate." She waited for a break in the boardwalk traffic and then jogged across to the sand. I picked up my flip-flops and broke into a run—and then took off. Yikes! The sand was burning hot. Aunt Elayne actually managed to run to the water faster than I did!

"Holy Christmas, that's cold!" Aunt Elayne held her shoes up higher so they didn't get clobbered by the spray. The surf rushed past our feet again, then back into the ocean, sinking us farther into the sand.

"I hear you're a runner," she said. The ocean was loud and she had to yell, even though she was only two feet away from me.

"Yeah," I answered. "Cross-country."

"You should run here!" There *were* all kinds of runners on the beach and on the boardwalk.

Athletes, definite nonathletes, older people, high school kids. But still, it wasn't how I usually ran.

"I don't usually run on sand—or barefoot!" I told her.

"Running is running," she answered. "Who cares how you do it?" She chased the surf a little as it receded. "Go on!" she ordered. "Go ahead. Run." She spread her hands out in both directions. I looked up and down the beach. To go right meant I had to run toward the Cyclone. I handed her my flip-flops and chose left.

"I'll meet you where the onion smell starts!" she called after me.

I was a little rusty and felt out of place, especially as I was wearing jean shorts and a long-sleeved T-shirt (the hospital is always so cold!), but I took off in a jog. I had only gone about three paces before I realized that I was still wearing Elayne's extra pair of sunglasses and they were bouncing up and down on my face. Not meant for running, that's for sure. I turned around to see my aunt still standing ankle deep in wet sand—watching after me. I jogged back, handed her the sunglasses, and jogged off again. "Onions!" she reminded me.

"Onions!" I called back. My mind started wandering, and I struggled to find a good pace. Then I reminded myself what I needed to do: keep my gaze up, breathe all the way into my stomach, use my arms. I didn't run very far—maybe a half mile—but it felt far enough. My legs felt sturdy again—useful— like they had when I had run in the stairwell, so much more familiar to me than my sitting legs. It felt good to have them back. And then I felt instantly, *instantly* guilty. Riley. Would Riley run again? Not that Riley was a big runner, but she deserved strong, steady legs. Was Elayne right? Would Riley never be the same? I made a U-turn and headed back, on familiar turf now. My heart was beating that great working-hard beat, and I caught a nod and a wave from a runner going in the opposite direction. Elayne saw Riley exactly as she was now without comparing her to the old one, like I did. I didn't want to admit it, but each morning on the way to the hospital, I wondered if this would be the day that Riley was back to old Riley. I took a hard right at a volleyball game and picked up the pace, mostly because the sand was so hot! The boardwalk wasn't much better. I didn't see Aunt Elayne on the boardwalk when I got there, but I did smell the onions. I did a slow-down jog down the ramp and found her at the ice-cream truck parked at the bottom.

"Ready?" she asked, a chocolate ice-cream cone in front of her mouth, framed by even bigger, fuller, crazier wind-whipped hair. Beach hair. She held out her ice cream as an offer. I declined.

"Ready." Was I?

"Lead the way," she said.

We walked off the elevator and right into my mother. Her face and neck were bright red. "Where have you been? Do you realize how long you've been gone?" She was frantic and grabbed my arm harder than I expected. "I've been looking all over for you! I told you to stay close to the building!"

"Leave the poor girl alone, will you, Paige?" Aunt Elayne waltzed right past my mother toward Riley's room, deliberately nudging her with her bag. A few of the nurses at the station stopped what they were doing.

"I'm *talking* to you, Elayne!" snapped my mom. "I just asked you a question. Where the hell have you been?"

"We took a walk to the beach," my aunt answered. It sounded a lot more casual than it actually was. Like we had a picnic or something.

"Oh, I see. Did you need a break from the hospital, is that it? Is this too hard for you?"

I had never heard my mother sound quite like that—it was something sharper than anger. But I felt responsible for Mom being mad at Aunt Elayne. I wanted to fix it. "C'mon Mom, stop," I pleaded, but she charged right past me toward her sister. "Aunt Elayne texted you!" I added.

My mother stopped short. "No, Aunt Elayne did *not* text me."

"What?" No wonder Mom was out of her mind.

"Oh, for Pete's sake, Paige. We went out for fresh air. You knew I was with her," Elayne said without turning around. That's when my mother grabbed her hard enough to spin her around.

"What the f—?" Aunt Elayne threw her arms up quickly, ready to defend herself or land the first blow. I couldn't tell.

One of the nurses looked up from his computer. "Ladies? Why don't we all take a deep breath?" He didn't wait for an answer, but nodded to someone else behind the desk, who picked up the phone.

"It's not her fault, Mom," I tried again. Well, it kinda was—why didn't my aunt text like she said? I even saw her with the phone. . . . Oh my gosh, that dog . . . that stupid dog!

"It *is* my fault." Elayne was practically nose to nose with my mother. "I dragged her out for a walk. I'm the one who wanted to get away. Mostly . . . from you!" She jabbed a finger at my mother.

"Me?" my mom shrieked. Then they really went at it, yelling over each other, their voices getting louder as the space between them got smaller and smaller. Now even the people at the far end of the hallway were staring at us. Those curious faces popping out of the doorways again. This time, they didn't duck back in.

"What the HELL is it now?" Aunt Maureen sprang out of Riley's room just as the security guard showed up. I cannot repeat the string of obscenities she muttered as she marched toward us. "I am sick to death of this! Sick of it! Do you know what your niece did all morning? She managed to stand up *on her own* and take a few steps with a walker! My daughter WALKED for the first time in a week—and instead of praying to God about how grateful I am, I have to listen to you two snipe at each other!" Riley used a walker today? *While I was at the beach?????*

The security guard took a step forward, but Aunt Maureen held up her hand to stop him. He stopped. "I love you both, but either find a way to get along or you can *both* go home!"

At that, Aunt Maureen stalked to the elevator without another word. The security guard held the door for her.

"Mo, stop, where are you going?" called my mom.

"To the F-BOMB chapel to get some F-BOMB peace!"

Aunt Maureen punched a button. Mom and Aunt Elayne stared at the closing doors, just as Riley peeked out of her own room, both hands on a walker to keep herself steady. Jodi, her physical therapist, was at her side.

The nurses' station broke out in a round of applause.

Riley took a bow.

DAY 8¾

There you are, Nora!" Monica was balancing a huge pile of paper and folders in her hands, and it was threatening to collapse. "I had an idea!"

Uh-oh. "What kind of idea?" The fish-tank chairs were already taken, so I was sitting on the couch closest to the little-kid art table with the crayons and construction paper. Yes, I was back in the PICU family room. I liked it better than the pediatric one, which was always crawling with kids. Monica sat on the other end of the couch, leaving a space between us for the pile, which I could now see had Riley's communication chart on top of it.

"Um, doesn't she need this?"

"She's with her OT[37] now." Monica began to spread papers and plastic sleeves on the cushion between us.

"Occupation? Like a job?"

"Kind of a weird title, right? Occupational therapy teaches people how to do everyday things for themselves—like brush their teeth or use a fork. Kinds of stuff we take for granted but have to be relearned by patients, especially after a stroke. OTs call them 'activities of daily living.'"[38]

"Oh."

"Anyway, her speech therapist told me that you had been working on something for Riley, and I thought you might be able to use some of this stuff." She popped open the metal rings on a hard red binder, the same kind I'd used for sixth-grade science, then picked up a plastic sheet protector and lined up the hole punches.

"What's this for?" I added a few more of the plastic sheets to the binder, even though I still had no idea why I was doing it.

"For . . . these." Monica now slid the hospital

---

[37] Reminder: occupational therapist.
[38] OTs usually call them "ADLs" for short.

word charts into the protectors. "Then you can add the ones you did and—if you want—keep adding new words and drawings, so everything is organized. It might make it easier for Riley, too, so it's all in one place. What do you think?" Her eyes were practically sparkling with excitement.

"Makes sense." I didn't have quite her enthusiasm about it—and I wasn't sure Riley would either. "You know that she doesn't . . . really . . . you know . . . use these so much, though?"

"Josephine mentioned that, but this is all new to Riley, so it may take some time. What's important is that it's there if she wants it."

"Yeah, okay." I found my drawings and words and carefully tore them out of the sketchbook, figuring out what order I should put them in. I also had drawings in my math notebook and on looseleaf paper I had in my summer work folder. Maybe organizing wasn't such a bad idea after all.

"I'll leave you to it." Monica stood, looking pleased. "If you think of anything else you need, just let me know. I have access to the office supplies," she said with a wink.

I smiled as she left. She was, without a doubt,

what my mother would call a "good egg." All good eggs should go in *The Official Riley Binder*, I decided.

Jack would definitely say Monica had a Fisher-Price quality to her, but I thought my drawing was okay, despite the fact that it made her look sort of disheveled, which she definitely was not. Of course, if Monica was in there, Josephine and Jodi should be too; and Dr. Mejia, but she should probably go at the top of the page, I thought. Hmm, this was going to require some planning. And what would I call the page? Helpers? Too preschool. Professionals? Boring. Specialists? That sounded depressing—who wants to see the entire team of specialists required to get you through the day and back on your feet? TEAM. Duh!

It took me more than an hour, but I thought Riley would be able to recognize everybody:

"Nora." This time it was Aunt Maureen who nudged me. "We need you."

I hadn't just fallen asleep on the PICU couch, I had spread myself all over it, like I was at home. "What's wrong?"

"Come on," she said, hauling me up. "We need you to play cards."

"What? With who?"

"Riley, silly. Your aunt Elayne is playing UNO with Riley to help her with her grip and her concentration." Confused, I shoved *The Official Riley Binder* into my backpack. *Did Riley want to play cards with me?* "Your aunt may be having a harder time than Riley!"

When we got to Riley's doorway, Aunt Maureen motioned for me to be quiet while we watched. Aunt Elayne cut the deck into two piles and held them vertically on the table in front of her, ready to shuffle. I could see from where I was that she was applying too much pressure, practically bending the cards in half. And then *PFFFFFFTTTTTT!* They were all over the place.

"How does a grown woman *not* know how to

shuffle a deck of cards?" Aunt Maureen teased. I picked three cards up off the floor, avoiding Riley's gaze. "Nora, honey, please help her, I can't watch anymore!" Aunt Elayne took a halfhearted swipe at her sister and then threw up her hands in mock defeat. This morning, Aunt Maureen was dropping F-bombs at her sister, and now they were acting like best friends at the lunch table.

I slid into the chair opposite Elayne and gathered up the sorry pile of cards—and then I stopped. I smelled coconut. The way it smelled on Riley's pillow at home. I put the cards down and stared at my cousin. Her hair was back! Her dark, thick, shiny, coconut-smelling hair was back! I gaped . . . and had to stop myself from grabbing a handful of it.

"She looks great, doesn't she?" Aunt Maureen was smiling ear to ear.

"She does!" I answered. Aunt Maureen jerked her head toward Riley. "I mean, you do! You look . . . awesome!" She did. She *really* did.

"Grat." Riley's face lit up—spark, spark, spark!—and she ran her fingers through her own hair. She was *feeling* more like herself. Not only did she have Riley hair again, but she was wearing purple sweatpants, and I could see her dark purple bra through the NY METS T-shirt she was wearing. Regular hair and a bra! There was no doubt she was smiling at me now—so close to being a full smile, an even smile. Maybe I'd been imagining that Riley was mad at me?

Aunt Elayne pointed to the curtain and then gave a thumbs-up sign to me. "New roommate," she mouthed.

I shuffled the UNO cards and dealt hands to Riley, Elayne, and me. It was turning out to be a good day—now Aunt Maureen was laughing with someone in the hallway.

"Free," said Riley. "Oh." She tugged on her blanket with her good hand. "Free-oh."

I threw down a green four.

"Free," said Riley, more forcefully. "Oh."

"Four," said Elayne. She rifled through the cards on the tray until she found a three. "This is a three," she said. "See the curves?"

"Per-oh," said Riley, turning to me. "Done Per-oh?"

"Pear? You're hungry?" asked Aunt Elayne. "You

want a pear? Of course, I'll get you something."

"She's cold," said a voice on the other side of the curtain. The new girl. "It's cold in here. She could probably use another blanket. And where's her dog?"

"See!!!" Riley shouted, her face pulling together and up into the biggest smile I had seen on her since the stroke. She almost looked like herself—her real self—her 100 percent self. Aunt Mo heard from the hallway and rushed back in as Aunt Elayne leaped up and slid the curtain wall back halfway. "What are you talking about?" she demanded to a very startled-looking girl in the other hospital bed.

"She's cold and she's looking for her dog."

"See, see, see!" Riley yelled. "Per, oh. Per, oh." I dropped my cards all over the floor.

"What?" Aunt Maureen looked from Riley to the girl to Riley again.

"*¿Dónde está el perro?*" the girl called out to Riley. I left the cards on the floor and pulled the sheet the rest of the way back so they could see each other.

"See, see!" said Riley. She pushed herself up with her good arm, then began gesturing wildly.

"See, see, see!" She was pointing at the girl like she had just won a prize on a game show.

Aunt Elayne looked back and forth between the girl and Riley. Aunt Maureen looked back and forth between the girl and Riley. We all looked back and forth between the girl and Riley. Even though I couldn't follow what they were saying, there was something familiar about the way they were speaking. It wasn't grunting or made-up words, and it wasn't gibberish. It was something real.

"Archie . . . is home . . . honey," said Aunt Maureen, like she wasn't quite sure she was using the right words. "Nora is taking very good care of him!"

"No, no," Riley answered. "No gooos meh." She shook her head and swung her good leg over the side of the bed toward the girl. Here was the one person in the world who seemed to understand what Riley was saying, and Riley seemed ready to crawl through hot lava to get to her. The girl swung her own legs over the side of the bed and dragged her monitor with her to move toward Riley. She looked closer to Riley's age than mine, and she was wearing pajamas instead of a hospital gown.

Her hair was dark blond—short, choppy, and dirty. Hospital hair. Definitely. Maybe even recently-in-the-PICU hair. She had the same *Beep beep beep.*

"No gooos meh." Riley shook her head harder and pointed at me. *Uh-oh.*

"¿No le gusta?" asked the girl. She gasped, then shot me a dirty look. I sensed a new triangle—and it wasn't a good one for me.

"See," said Riley, shaking her head.

"She says you don't like the dog?" the girl now asked me, her voice accusatory. *In English.* In English. So—my mind was exploding—so: Riley was still in there. Riley was having a conversation. *In Spanish.* "It's Spanish!" I yelled.

"¡¡¡¡¡SÍ!!!!!" Riley snort-laughed. *"¡¡SÍ SÍ SÍ SÍ SÍ!!"*

"Duh," said the girl. She towered over me, with a *you're stupid* look on her face. I narrowed my eyes at her. Oh yeah, we were in full triangle. *Well, I'm on the team and you're not!*

"Free-oh?" asked Aunt Maureen.

"What on Earth . . . ," said Aunt Elayne.

"F-R-Í-O," said the girl, with a shrug. "Cold."

"Pear?"

"P-E-R-R-O," said the girl. "Dog."

"See?"

"S-Í," I answered this one for her. "Yes."

"*Sí, sí, sí,*" Riley said. She slapped the bed with her good hand. "*¡¡Síííííí!!*"

"You knew I was tomato soupin' the dog?" I yelped. The girl shot me another dirty look. Was I really the only kid in the world who didn't like dogs?

"*Sí, sí,*" Riley whispered. "*Sopa. Sí.*"

"'*Sopa*'?" asked Aunt Maureen.

"Soup," said the girl. "I don't get it."

I got it. The "tomato" part was implied.

Aunt Elayne sat back down slowly and looked at Aunt Maureen. But Aunt Maureen was looking at Riley, and Riley was still looking at the girl. Nobody was looking at me.

"Yamma?" Riley asked the girl.

"Sophia," said the girl. "*¿Cómo se llama?*"

"Rye," she answered. "Yammo Rye."

"*Hola,* Rye." Sophia smiled.

"O, Sofe."

Riley waved her mother over closer to Sophia. "Moo-Moo . . . Sofe." She was introducing them!

"Hi, Sophia," answered Aunt Mo, looking

stunned, but remembering her manners. "How are you, honey? You can call me Maureen."

"Moo-Moo," corrected Riley.

"Moo-Moo works too," said my aunt.

"Moo-Moo . . . *casa*," said Riley in a firm voice, pointing at Sophia, then her mom.

Sophia shook her head, embarrassed.

"*¡Sí!*" insisted Riley. "*Sí. Ca-sa.*"

"What is it?" asked Aunt Maureen.

"She said," Sophia said hesitantly. "She said she wants you to go home."

Oh.

Maybe Riley wanted some privacy after all.

DAY 8%10

Riley—or Rye, as Sophia called her—was like a new person. It was as if she'd been talking underwater this whole time and had finally broken through to the surface. Apparently, stored in the language part of Riley's brain were a few boxes of Spanish[39] she must have packed away in there from school. Aunt Maureen even joked about how apparently Riley's brain clearly knew more Spanish than Riley had let on, because Riley gotten a C in it on her last report card. Still, Riley

---

[39] Of course, plenty of the doctors and nurses at the hospital spoke Spanish but had never thought to speak Spanish with Riley, just as they'd never thought to randomly communicate with her in Russian or Mandarin. It is rare for your brain to spit out another language after a stroke, head injury, or coma, but it does happen.

was not speaking good, clear Spanish, so Sophia had her work cut out for her.[40]

"Verano," Sophia said across Riley's bed. "V-E-R-A-N-O. Summer." She was helping me translate the drawings I had done into Spanish. Riley sometimes tried to repeat the words after Sophia said them. I think it was a good exercise for her. It was a little weird—and I was a little jealous—that Sophia, a complete stranger, seemed to be an even more important part of Riley's team than I was. Even my "team-ness" had been out-triangled.

"Abraham Lincoln." She laughed. She had beautiful, perfect white teeth, like Riley's. "A-B-R-A—"

"I got it, I got it!" I laughed right back. You are who you are in any language. Sophia, if you looked at her, seemed pretty healthy, just a little pale and tired. There was no cast, no bandages, and no loud phone calls, so I had no idea what her story was. Her mom, Ofelia, came late in the afternoon. Thanks to Jack, I figured she must be coming when she got off work.

[40] The best news was that it was also likely that her English wouldn't be far behind her Spanish. It was a sure sign her brain was really picking up steam—just not in the order you might expect.

Riley looked over her new words:

Summer
VERANO

Tamarin
Monkey
TAMARIN
MONO

Owl
BÚHO

Fries
PAPAS
FRITAS

NY Mets
METS DE
NUEVA YORK

Abe
Lincoln
ABE
LINCOLN

"Can I have a sheet of paper?" Sophia asked.

I ripped one out for her.

She took the pencil out of my hand. Riley and I watched, both of us, I think, expecting her to write something, but instead she began to sketch.

"What's that?" I asked.

"You'll see," replied Sophia without looking up. She had a tube taped to her hand, too, and it ran to the IV pole she had rolled beside her. She turned the page as she drew, which was something Riley never did, making it harder to see what she was drawing. Finally, there was this:

HORSE / CABALLO

"When is Riley going to use the word 'horse'?" I asked, without complimenting her on what was a pretty great-looking horse.

"Maybe right after she uses the word 'wolf,'" Sophia answered. Wow. It was like that? Really? I reached to take the pencil back. "I'm not done." And she wasn't. A cat appeared on the page in under a minute. She labeled it *Gato* and *Slipper*.

"Slipper? What language is that?"

"That's his name, silly. That's my cat!"

Riley petted the stupid cat on the page. "Ola, Slips." Ugh. They were so annoying now. And guess what? These weren't Riley words, they were Sophia words. How did that help anybody? I decided I was going to disqualify the page and rip it out later when nobody was around.

"One more," Sophia announced. She kept the page still this time and started to sketch eyes, topped with thick brows (they looked like caterpillars to me, just saying) and then, in astonishing speed, finished a face that I did not recognize. She didn't label it either.

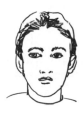

I pointed at the dark-haired guy on the page. "Do I even know this person?"

"*Sí,*" Riley said, then grinned *and* nodded an exaggerated nod. Her personality was catching up with her hair.

"Should I give Nora a hint?" Sophia laughed.

Sí, laugh, *sí*, laugh, *sí*, laugh.

"He's *really* cute. . . ."

Laugh, laugh, laugh.

"Random cute guy? Seriously? How could you both know the same random cute guy? That's impossible!"

"Night shift!" said Sophia. I guess Spanish wasn't the only thing that Sophia and Riley knew and I didn't. "Riley really likes him," she teased.

Riley shook her head.

"¡Usted!" She pointed at Sophia. *"¡Usted!"* Sophia answered her back in a string of Spanish and Riley almost fell out her bed, she was laughing so hard. I waited for Sophia's translation, but it never came.

"So . . . anyway," I interrupted. "Do you guys want to play UNO?"

"Um, sure," said Sophia. Riley shrugged.

I shuffled my expert shuffle and dealt the hand just as Sophia's mom, Ofelia, walked into the room.

"Hola," she said. "Time to rest, my love." Her mother was right. Sophia had circles under her eyes, and she was beginning to slump in her chair.

I didn't think she needed help walking back to her bed, but her mom held her by the arm, anyway, and then gently closed the curtain between us.

"Just us, I guess," I said to Riley.

"No." She laid her cards down on the table. *"No más."*

"She said 'no more,'" Sophia called—uninvited— over the curtain. "She doesn't want to play."

"Yeah, I got that." I collected the cards I had already dealt and put the deck back in the box. "So, do you really like that nurse? The cute one?"

"No," Riley said, looking out the window into the hallway. She waved at her mother, who was almost always close by, even if she wasn't in the room.

"Can I get you anything?" I tried.

"Nuh-uh." Even Sophia realized that no translation was necessary. Either that, or she was asleep. Whatever.

"Maybe we can . . ." I stopped. Riley's eyelids were heavy and the shadows were back on her face. I guess they even *slept* at the same time. Hospital BFFs. I kicked at my backpack on the floor. Sticking out of the top was the corner of the Abraham

Lincoln biography. I held it up and Riley smiled. I picked a random page and read out loud. "'The initial Northern responses to the Emancipation Proclamation were predictable. Antislavery men were jubilant. "God bless Abraham Lincoln," exclaimed Horace Greeley's *New York Tribune.* "The president," announced Joseph Medill's *Chicago Tribune*, had promulgated "the grandest proclamation ever issued by a man."'"[41]

Translate that, Sophia.

I needed Jack to help me find more words so Sophia didn't take over my word board. I still felt a little funny taking the elevator up to the PICU family room, but Jack said it wasn't like I was sneaking in to steal doughnuts from sick people.

"How's she doing?" Audra asked when I walked past the PICU nurses' station.

"She's good!" I replied, flashing her a smile. Riley *was* good. And I mean like 65 percent Riley good. The stuff that mattered. She was practicing using her walker (and Jodi) and even managing

---

[41] Quote from *Lincoln*. Copyright © 1995 by David Herbert Donald. All rights reserved.

her own ADLs, like using a fork and brushing her teeth. But what I wanted, and I know I'm a jerk, but what I really wanted was to be the one who understood her the best—that's why I needed Jack. We had only been off the floor a few days, and already there were new faces in the family room, including the one sitting next to Jack in front of the fish tank. Oh. I was too far into the room to pretend to be going someplace else, and besides, Jack saw me and waved me over.

"Hey," he said. "How's it going?"

"Hey," I answered. I stood awkwardly to the side of the fish tank. The kid in the chair didn't look up. "What's going on?"

"Same old stuff," he said, pulling an ottoman over for me to sit. I declined. "This is Jeremy."

"Hi, Jeremy." Protocol dictated that I did not open the conversation by asking Jeremy who he was visiting in the pediatric intensive care unit or why. From the terrified look on his face, though, it had to be somebody close to him and for something pretty serious. He also looked young—younger than Jack and younger than me. I scanned the room but didn't see anybody who he might belong to.

"Jeremy and I were just talking about the fish," Jack continued, just cheerfully enough to not sound annoying. "Jeremy likes Batman for the blue one and Joker for the yellow one." Superhero names. This kid was even younger than he looked—possibly too young to be left alone in the family room with strangers, was what my mother would have said. But clearly, emergency rules were at work. "Solid choices, I told him," Jack added.

"Great names," I agreed.

"Thanks." Jeremy seemed to brighten at this. I exchanged looks with Jack, letting him know I wanted to talk to him, but it was clear he was going to stick with the kid. I wondered if that was a pattern with Jack—befriend the new kid by the fish tank. The awkward silence that followed made me realize that they had been talking before I barged in—maybe even about why Jeremy was here—and perhaps I should wait for a better time to vent about Riley's extremely helpful and bilingual roommate. The only other kid in the room was a five-year-old girl coloring Elmo bright green at the art table with her mother.

I had left my backpack in the room, so I

borrowed some paper from the art table, sat down on the ottoman Jack had offered, and worked on some words that Riley and I had in common.

Harry Potter   skateboarding[42]

doughnuts

Every time somebody walked past the glass wall, Jeremy looked up, but he didn't say a word. It seemed just as rude to interrupt the silence as it had been to interrupt the conversation. I finally gave up on a graceful exit and stood.

"I'll check in with you guys later," I announced, feeling very much replaced again.

---

[42] Okay, neither of us actually knew how to skateboard, but we talked about it a lot and we *planned* on doing it and even knew the skate park where we were going to go. Someday. When at least one of us had a skateboard.

"Okay." Jack half smiled and waved, but Jeremy just blinked at me. I think the poor kid was in shock. Out in the hallway, I ran into the dad version of Jeremy—he had an equally terrified look on his face.

"Excuse me, which way is the—" he began.

"Family room? It's down the hallway, on the right." I gestured. "There's food in there too," I added for no reason; I just wanted to say something helpful. I pushed the button for the elevator and watched him stride into the family room, straightening up a bit, I thought, before facing his son, exchanging his scared look for something stronger, something in control, something that would make his son less afraid.

The elevator was taking too long—and I remembered the stairs—and I wanted to feel my legs move again. I disappeared through the stairwell door and this time ran all the way to the ground floor. I was sure Jack was introducing himself to Jeremy's dad—and maybe showing him where the coffee was and how to turn on the television, going out of his way to be useful. I thought of Firefighter Dad trading cotton candy with his son helping

Riley and directing us to the hospital. I thought of the woman who called us a cab. And the couple who stepped aside so we could get into it. Maybe Sophia drawing a horse and a cat wasn't that much of a crisis after all.

At the second-floor landing, I stepped aside for a group of people in scrubs, talking casually as they walked up the steps. When I hit the ground floor, I pivoted and started right back up at the same pace until my hamstrings told me otherwise. I hadn't stretched in over a week, and I felt it. Most of the hamstring stretches I knew were on the floor—and that seemed gross. So I walked the remaining flights back up to pediatrics, making a mental note to stretch when I got home.

And maybe run again tomorrow.

Aunt Maureen cried a million tears and had half a dozen false exits before she finally left the hospital that night. She and my mom chatted in the kitchen for an hour when we got home, even though I knew they were both dead tired. I was finally glad Riley's room was wide open, because

I got to hear them talking and laughing, like it was just a regular summertime sister visit. When I finally climbed into bed and swung my legs up . . . OUCH.

I slid onto the floor and stretched.

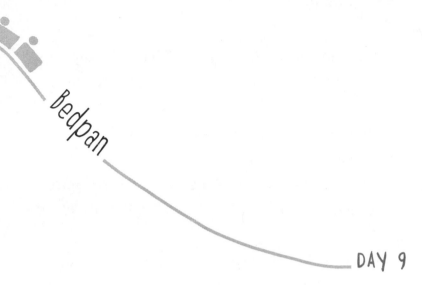

Bedpan

DAY 9

eady?" Dr. Mejia smiled broadly at Aunt Maureen and then looked specifically at Riley. "We have a meeting with the social worker about getting you home by the end of the week. I'll bring your mom back in half an hour or so." Home. Finally. All those sparks really did add up to progress. Enough progress to send 80 percent Riley home.

"Moo-Moo," Riley said as Aunt Mo followed the doctor out, but she was okay with her mom leaving. It was just her way of saying, *See you later, Mom.*

"I'm going downstairs for an after-breakfast cigarette," Aunt Elayne announced next. What? She was leaving? Leaving me alone with Riley?

"I think you're supposed to stay until Mom gets back from the cafeteria," I said carefully. "Riley shouldn't be alone."

"She won't be alone," she answered. Her hair was already in the hallway. "You're here."

"But . . . um . . . I think a *grown-up* is supposed to be here," I called after her. "Or at least close by . . ."

Riley made a tiny wave with her good arm.

"See, Riley's fine with it," my aunt said from the hall. "So you'll be fine too. I won't be gone long." And then she was. Gone. I hadn't been alone with Riley since . . . well, since the safety bar came down on the roller coaster.

"So . . . ? You want some water or something?"

"No, gras."

"I do!" Sophia called softly from the other side of the sheet. Jeez, was she always listening? "My pitcher is empty!" I jerked the curtain back, annoyed, but Sophia looked so much sicker—now in her bed—than she had just yesterday. She was losing sparks. I carried Riley's water pitcher around the curtain and poured Sophia a cup. Her hands shook when she held it to her mouth. I waited for her to finish, then took the empty cup from her and put it on her table.

"Gracias," she whispered.

"De nada," I whispered back. I stood for a few moments, just in case she wanted more. I wondered if Riley knew what my mom had told me about Sophia—that she may need a pacemaker to help regulate her heart. Did they talk about that kind of stuff?

When I sat down, Riley looked me straight in the face and said, "Orb."

"Orb?" There was no translation from Sophia. Was she asleep already?

Riley put her hands together to mimic an open book, like in charades. "Orb," she insisted. She searched around the bed and table, now littered with paperwork and magazines. "AHA!" She found what she wanted . . . the red binder Monica helped me make . . . *The Official Riley Binder*!

"The ORB!" I exclaimed. Man, she was closer to 90 percent! No wonder they were sending her home.

She found her way to the hospital chart and stabbed her finger at:

BATHROOM / BAÑO

"Oh. Okay. I'll call the nurse," I said.

She shook her head. Okay then.

We always left the room when she signaled to Aunt Maureen, so I pointed to the bedpan on the chart.

BEDPAN / ORINAL DE CAMA

Riley shook her head no.

"How about I just get the nurse for you?" I suggested. "Does she, uh, help you with that?" I had no idea how this worked.

"No. No," she said. She pointed to the bathroom in the corner and then to the picture again.

"You want to use the actual bathroom? Do you want me to get your mom?" Maybe Riley was a little embarrassed to have a nurse take her to the bathroom. I'd definitely be!

Riley frowned. She pointed at me and then again at the bathroom. She didn't want to wait for her mother. She wanted *me* to take her to the *bathroom*. She was already getting in position to swing her legs over. If I didn't help her, I swear, I think she was going to try to do it herself.

"Can you . . . can you do that? Are you allowed? What are we going to do with your, uh, wires and . . . stuff?" I asked. She blinked at me. Dumb! We both knew she couldn't answer a string of complicated questions like that! I'd have to figure it out myself. The bathroom wasn't that far away— five or six steps from the end of Riley's bed. She used her good hand to make the walking motion with her pointer and middle fingers.

"Like physical therapy?" When they walked, the wires and IV drip rolled along with them. She nodded.

"Okay. *Sí.* Yes," I said. I circled around to the other side of the bed, where her IV drip and her monitor were. I'd seen Jodi work with her to get up and sit down, and walk the hallway, all with the pole rolling behind them. I was pretty sure I knew what to do. Still . . .

"Are you sure?" I asked.

Riley gave me a thumbs-up.

Then she reached over and pulled apart a small box I hadn't seen before. The numbers on her monitor went dark, the lines went flat, and my own heart did triple beats.

"What are you doing?! You need that! We need that!"

Riley shook her head, making the walking motion with her fingers again. "Jo."

"You don't use that when you walk with Jodi?"

"No." She smiled. I was terrified she was going to rip the IV needle right out of her hand too, but she didn't.

"Okay, ready?" I pulled the covers back and she swung her legs over the side of the bed. She had gotten pretty good at that. She took a deep breath and I thought—I hoped—she was going to change her mind. But she didn't. She reached her good leg down until her foot touched the floor, then very, very slowly followed with her stroke leg. She motioned for me to stand in front of her. Feet apart, I remembered. Jodi repeated it every time they stood up together. I checked to make sure Riley had a wide stance. She did. Okay. Good start. I put my leg in front of hers, so her knee couldn't buckle.

"Shoot!" I'd forgotten to bring the walker closer to the bed. It was up against the wall, under the corridor window. I stretched one arm out, but I couldn't reach it and support Riley at the same time. "Wait, sit down a second . . . the walker . . ."

"No. Me." Riley put her arm up around my shoulder.

"Riley, the walker. You need it!"

"Me. You." I didn't want to do this. But I didn't want to let her down. We could certainly make it five steps together, couldn't we?

"On the count of three, we pivot, okay? We need to turn your body toward the bathroom," I said. "Ready?"

"*Sí,*" she said.

"One, two . . . oops . . . *Uno, dos, tres.*" She shuffled her feet and I shuffled with her. We were in position to walk straight ahead to the bathroom. I was on her strong side and the bed was on her weaker side. She swayed a little bit, but I pulled her closer. She felt solid, heavy. I remembered her weight pressing on me in the roller-coaster car. "Okay, now we're going to step forward. On the count of three. *Uno, dos, tres."* We stepped.

"Me. You. See?"

"Again," I said. *"Uno, dos, tres."* Step. I pulled the pole along and we shuffled another step forward.

"Free-o." Riley giggled.

"Cold?"

She looked down.

"Your feet?"

She nodded. She was barefoot. "Should I put your slippers on?" She shook her head. I think she wanted to just keep going. Could she get sick this way? I'm sure the floor was kind of gross. If Aunt Maureen walked in and saw her bare feet, I think she'd probably freak out. I know it was freaking me out, but Riley seemed okay with it, so I let it go.

It might have only been about six steps to the bathroom from the edge of the bed, but I hadn't accounted for Riley steps. Hers were much smaller than they used to be. And every step took a lot out of her. Six steps quickly grew into twelve and then fifteen small half step-and-rolls. She was sweating. And her face had gone a little gray, I noticed with alarm. She no longer had the bed on her left side, either. It was all floor. I should have put a chair in that space to give her something to lean against besides me. Too late, but I could do it on the way back.

Three more shuffles. We were still barely halfway there. "Do you want to turn around?" I asked. I *really* wished a grown-up was here. She shook her head fiercely, so we kept going. "Stay with me," I said, repeating what Marisol always said to me during the worst part of a run, when the initial adrenaline had worn off and the finish line was still impossibly far away. "Stay with me."

Inch by inch, we shuffled, two feet away, one foot. Out of habit, I looked up to check her vitals— her HR, her BP—but there was no monitor for reassurance; it stood next to her bed, with its connection dangling free. *This could not have been a good idea.*

We were a mere step away from the door—the

closed door. Grrrr! Why did I not think this through? We were in our own way! "Okay, Riley. The door opens outward into the room, so I'm going to come around in front of you and then we are going to pivot, so you can lean against the wall and I will stay in front of you. Got it?" I parked the pole out of the way of the door.

"*Sí, sí . . .*" She needed to sit down. I came in front of her, like Jodi did when she helped Riley stand up, and hugged my arms around her waist, grabbing my own hands behind her to support her until her back was against the wall. "I've got you, so you can lean into me if you need to. I'm going to let go and open the door with one hand. *Uno, dos, tres.*"

We did it! We made it! The bathroom walls were lined with grab bars, just like the PICU bathroom, and Riley grabbed ahold of one as soon as she could. I let go of her for a second. She held herself steady, both hands on a rail. I pulled the IV pole closer and then shut the door and hurried back, my arms under her armpits now, and helped her lower herself onto the toilet. Now *I* was sweating and *my* heart was racing. But we did it! We did it!!

"Uhhh . . . oh." Riley looked down at her legs; she was still wearing sweatpants! We had been so excited about getting her on the toilet that we forgot some of the basic rules of peeing.

"Do you, um, want me to . . ." I really didn't want to say "pull down your pants" out loud.

"No." She stopped me with wide eyes.

"Okay," I said, almost giddy with relief. "I'll be right outside the door. Just call out when you're done."

"No," she said. She held her open hand in front of her.

"No? You want me to help?" I asked. We didn't have a lot of words in here. No Sophia, no ORB.

"*Perro,*" she said, and opened her hand again.

"Dog?"

She opened her hand again.

"Stay? Are you telling me to stay—like a dog??"

"Yessi," she grunt-laughed.

"Oh my God." I laughed as well. "I can't believe you!" So I made the hand signal for *sit*. "Good dog!" I patted her on the head.

Riley made her laughing sound again and motioned for me to turn around. We've never actually used the bathroom at the same time. We'd held the door for each other sometimes, when the lock on a stall didn't work, but even then, just listening felt embarrassing to me, though, of course, Riley would say, *It's perfectly natural, everybody pees!* This was different. Helping a sick person go to the bathroom is not the same as laughing outside a stall at the movie theater. It's not the same at all. I heard a strange *zhhipping*, and she started to pee. I was so proud of her!

"K," she said. I turned around but then I wasn't sure where to look, because I didn't want to stare at her sitting on the toilet bowl, but more importantly, I didn't want her to think that I thought it was gross to be in there. I stared at a spot a foot above her head. Seeing her without looking at her. I heard pee again, so I guess she hadn't been finished after all. When it stopped, I looked down at her face. *Her* eyes were closed. Maybe she didn't want to see me watching her pee. I should have closed my eyes. She was pulling up her sweatpants with one hand. Hard to watch. Even harder to do. I took a step forward to help, but she held up her hand. *Stay.*

Riley tried to say something that sounded like "pup." *Up?*

"Okay, I'll help you up," I said. But she didn't wait for me. She leaned forward to stand, but her feet were too close together. And then it happened. Riley lost her balance. She reached for the support rail and missed, grabbing at me and pulling us both down to the floor. I fell right on top of her. Her head practically bounced off the tile floor.

Oh my God. Oh my God. Oh my God. "Riley! Riley!" I saw the emergency button on the wall next to the toilet and lunged for it, pressing it over and over again. "Help!! Help!!" I was screaming at the top of my lungs. "Riley! Riley! Are you okay?" She was looking at me, but she didn't answer. Her eyes were big and scared, and she started thrashing around on the floor. "RILEY!!!!!!!!" Blood was everywhere, a pool of it forming beneath her, my own hands covered in it as I tried to calm her.

The bathroom door flew open and someone pushed me out of the way and crouched over Riley. I wriggled underneath the sink, closing my eyes as tightly as I could.

"I need help in here!" the woman bellowed.

Two people in scrubs came running in. They lifted Riley up off the floor and carried her back to her bed. The bathroom door closed behind them.

"She was on the floor," I heard somebody say.

"Riley, Riley? Look at me, honey." Dr. Mejia's voice. Dr. Mejia was here.

But Riley didn't answer. She didn't even *beep*.

I curled into the fetal position, stunned. Did Riley hit her head when she fell? She did. I know she did. Did I manage to knock another blood clot loose? I curled into a tighter ball. Riley was right. The floor was cold, and now covered in blood.

"There you go, honey," Dr. Mejia was saying. "There you go. It's all right."

I pressed my face against my knees and began to cry. And cry and cry.

At some point, I heard a tap at the door. I ignored it. Then again, harder. "Nora? It's okay." It was Sophia's mom. I still didn't answer. "She's okay," she assured me. "I'm coming in?" She slowly pulled the door open and crouched down on the floor. "Everything is okay. Her IV line came out. . . . She's okay."

I stared at the IV pole too. Hanging and dripping,

splashes of blood beneath it, where the fall had yanked it right out of her hand.

"She wanted to use the bathroom," I said, choking back a sob. I wiped my face and flinched at the smell of urine. That wetness, it was under me. I rolled over and stared. I'd been lying on a wet diaper. Oh, Riley. No wonder you wanted to use the real bathroom. How long had it been wet? And how long had she been wanting to take it off? I pulled it out from under me and Sophia's mom took it and tossed it in the garbage without a word. "Clean yourself up and let's get you something else to wear." She washed her hands, pulled the pole out with her, and shut the door.

I washed my own hands; they were still trembling as I ran some paper towels under the faucet, covered them with the pink, foamy soap, and cleaned myself off, all the while fuming at how stupid, STUPID I was. "Pup" was "paper"—*toilet paper.* That's what Riley had been trying to say. The toilet paper roll was new, and she couldn't undo it. That's what she had needed. I was so stupid. I turned on the faucet and washed my hands again. Riley—she hadn't washed her hands. I tossed the paper towel in the trash on top of the diaper. Riley hadn't been embarrassed to pee in front of me; she was embarrassed by the diaper. I was ashamed to admit that I was embarrassed too. I'd spent so much time looking at her face and her trembling and trying to understand her speech. Those seemed like the biggest struggles to me. I hadn't thought about something as basic as using the bathroom. Or worse, not being able to use it.

Sophia's mom was at the door again. "Nora, I have some scrubs for you." She really knew her way around a hospital, that's for sure. "Probably a little big, but they'll do." I opened the door just wide enough for her to hand them to me.

"Thanks," I mumbled. I put the scratchy blue scrubs on and pulled the string as tight as it would go on the pants. They were huge. Then I grabbed a few more paper towels for Riley and ran them under the water with some soap.

When I came out, soggy paper towels in hand, Mom and Aunt Maureen were back. "Nora, what on Earth happened?" Aunt Maureen said, gaping at me. Sophia was out of her bed and standing next to her mother.

"Why are you wearing those?" Mom asked, "and where's Elayne?" I walked past them both without saying a word and sat down in my regular chair next to Riley, feeling jittery again. Sophia's mom caught my eye and then closed the curtain.

Dr. Mejia motioned for the grown-ups to wait for her out into the hallway, telling them she'd join them in a minute. One of the nurses had stayed behind too, redoing an IV pole and reattaching the monitor contacts to Riley.

Dr. Mejia turned to me. "Nora, I know you are upset, but I need you to tell me what happened, and how it happened."

Still hiccuping from the cry, I did my best to explain. Dr. Mejia nodded thoughtfully, wanting every detail until I was finally done. "That is all good to know, Nora. That is important. Thank you." She shifted her attention to Riley. "Riley, because of your blood thinners,[43] we need to be extra careful about falls, cuts, and bruises. I had discussed this with your mother before, and I'm

---

[43] Blood thinners are very common for people who have had strokes because they prevent the blood from forming new clots. But it also makes for an awful lot of bleeding from even minor things—like an IV needle being yanked out of your arm.

251

sorry not to have mentioned it to you earlier, but you are at high risk for internal bleeding. We'll need to do a CT scan right away and then a few more over the next twenty-four to thirty-six hours. Do you understand?" Riley nodded. "I'm going to now go to talk to your mother about it, okay?"

Riley looked stunned. "I'm so sorry, Riley," I said the moment the doctor was gone. "Are you okay?"

"*Sí,*" she said. "*Sí.*"

"It's all my fault," I said. "I'm sorry."

She shook her head.

Beep. Beep. Beep.

"I'm sorry for all of it," I choked out. I wanted to say more, but she shook her head again, this time reaching out and squeezing my hand. I didn't know if she was comforting me, or if she was just too tired to talk, or if she was hurt all over again. I waited to see if there was something else she wanted to tell me, but she stayed quiet too.

"We forgot to wash your hands," I said at last. I took her good hand in mine and washed it with the paper towels. Then I took her trembling stroke hand, and as gently as I could, washed that one too.

Dr. Mejia sailed back into the room. "We are going to take you down for that CT scan now, Riley."

"You're an old pro at those by now, right, sweetheart?" Aunt Maureen assured her, coming in behind the doctor. She was making an effort not to sound upset. Riley nodded, but she looked scared. "I'm going to take the ride with you and wait," her mother added, just as two orderlies arrived to wheel Riley down, taking a nurse with them. Aunt Maureen wouldn't even glance my way when she followed the bed out. I didn't have much time to worry about that, though, because Elayne arrived with a tray of coffee less than a minute later—and my mother pounced.

"How could you leave them alone, Elayne? What were you thinking? Do you know what you've done?"

"What happened? What's wrong?" Elayne set the tray of coffee down and stepped farther into the room. That was brave. I would have backed away if Mom was shrieking at me like that.

"They just took Riley down for a CT scan. She fell in the bathroom—the doctors are worried about internal bleeding!"

"Oh no," cried Aunt Elayne, now backing away. "Oh no . . ."

"Oh yes, thanks to you," my mother finished between clenched teeth. She looked angrier than I had ever seen her. "You couldn't stay here for ten minutes? TEN MINUTES??"

Elayne knelt down on the floor in front of me, clearly shaken. "I'm so sorry, Nora." Her voice was quivering. "I never should have left you. . . ."

"But you did," my mom seethed. "It was too much to ask! It's just like Mom all over again. Show up late, make an appearance, and stay as far away as possible! Only this time, Riley has to pay the price. As if that poor girl hasn't been through enough."

Elayne sat back on the floor and pressed her head into her knees. "What did I do?" She began to rock back and forth on the floor in front of me. I was worried that she was more than just upset, she was on the edge of something. Mom continued to glare, a cold, hard glare, at her sister. It was the only time I'd ever seen her not comfort someone who needed it.

"I can't even look at you, Elayne," she finally said in disgust. "Nora, come on, let's go."

I couldn't get my thoughts straight, let alone my words. I walked around Elayne. She was crying silently now. My mother was already in the hallway—moving away from her sister, again. I knelt down next to my aunt and put my arms around her. She and I were in *this* triangle together. "It's not your fault," I said. "It's mine. All of it."

She broke into full sobs while my mother stormed back in to grasp my arm and drag me away.

We stayed at the hospital that night, my mom and me, even after we found out that the CT scan was clear. Riley didn't return to the eighth floor—they put her back in the PICU for the night. The medicine she was on—blood thinners—did exactly what it sounded like, so if she got hurt, or even had a bruise, her blood would flow much more quickly, and that was a problem. Dr. Mejia explained that the worry was a "delayed hemorrhage"—an internal bleed that might not show up immediately—and they would be better equipped to monitor her in the PICU. Two days of clear scans and she'd be allowed to go back to the eighth floor. I desperately wanted to see Riley, but Aunt Maureen was "emotionally exhausted," my mother said, and wanted time alone with Riley that night.

As much as I had missed being in the PICU family room, rather than the pediatric one, I didn't want to *have* to be back here. Mom conked out in one of the big chairs, but I barely slept. I worried about Riley and I worried about Aunt Elayne, too, by herself in a hotel and feeling sick with guilt. I knew the feeling. Nobody had yelled at me, nobody had lectured me. Elayne was the target this time—a target nobody had when Riley had had the stroke, but only because nobody knew the target should have been me. Nobody but Riley, that is, but her post-stroke memory was unreliable—if she had remembered the Cyclone morning briefly a few days ago, it was gone now.

After breakfast, twelve hours after Riley fell, Aunt Mo said Mom and I could see her now. I sprinted down the hall.

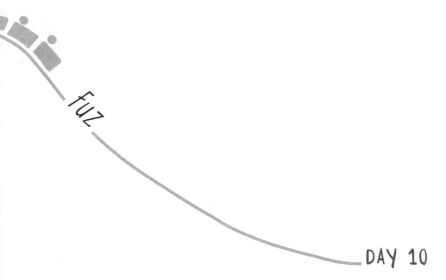

Riley pushed herself right up with her good arm when she saw us.

"Hey," I said.

"Hey." She was wide-eyed and now sitting up straight.

"Are you okay, sweetheart?" asked my mother. She tried to hold Riley's hand, but Riley shook it off. She didn't want to be babied.

"Skay," she said.

"Good," said my mom, taking the hint. "How are *you* doing?" she asked her sister. Aunt Maureen felt worse than Riley, if the purple rings below her eyes were any indication.

"Weird to be back here again," said Aunt Mo.

"We shouldn't be back here at all," fumed my mother, looking as angry as Aunt Mo looked tired. "Is it really so hard to be the adult and sit in a room?" Aunt Maureen avoided my mother's eye, but that didn't stop her tirade. "Maybe Elayne will have enough sense to head back to California now. I swear she does more harm than good. Why is she even here?"

"Not now, Paige, please," Aunt Maureen pleaded. "Not now."

"Em here." Riley was leaning forward on her bed, reaching toward my mother. "Em here."

"Huh?" I thought there was some Riley Spanish in there, but without Sophia, I was lost. Riley laid her hand on her chest. "Em here," she repeated. She looked to me for help. *Em here. Em here.*

"I'm here," I announced. "She's saying 'I'm here.' I think she means Aunt Elayne is here because Riley is here. She's here for Riley." Now my mother began fidgeting with her handbag, looking embarrassed. I avoided looking at her.

"ORB," said Riley. She wasn't quite finished with the conversation. I fished it out of my bag. Riley went straight to the family page, presumably to say something else about Aunt Elayne. She looked confused for half a second—and then she snickered. Not laughed, not smirked, not smiled, but definitely *snickered*.

"What is it?" Her mother leaned in and Riley turned the page toward her. Aunt Maureen did not snicker—she burst out laughing and then quickly covered her mouth.

"What? What's so funny?" My mom and I spoke at the same time—and then I saw it. Aunt Elayne's work for sure!

Aunt Paige

Mom went purple. She grabbed the ORB out of Riley's hands, but Riley reached up and grabbed it right back!

"M-m-mine," Riley said, placing her hand on her chest. "M-m-m-mine." Her heart rate was up a tick.

"She's right, Paige," said Aunt Maureen, trying hard not to laugh. "It is *her* book."

"It's not funny, Maureen," argued my mother, even more uncomfortable now at the receiving end of Elayne's prank. "Elayne was completely irresponsible yesterday and—"

"And that was yesterday, Paige," answered Aunt Maureen, no longer laughing. "And—it wasn't *entirely* her fault either," she added, shooting looks at both Riley and me. I braced myself for her to say more, but nothing came.

"But Mo—"

"But nothing, Paige." Aunt Maureen was done with it—case closed. Riley's eyes had been bouncing between the two of them, but she stopped, confident that her mother had had the last word. Riley's attention was on the notebook again.

"Uh-oh," she said, angling it toward me so I could get a better look, and cupping the drawings for privacy. Oh. That. I hadn't had a chance to share that page with Riley yet.

There were no labels in either English or Spanish. Riley caught my eye and raised one eyebrow—a skill I had completely forgotten she had. Riley got it.

"Fuz, hep, jay," she said matter-of-factly.

Our mothers were staring at the page, clueless.

Aunt Maureen leaned back into her chair, a flash of recognition registering on her face.

"Huh?" My mother was still lost. Riley let out a heavy sigh.

"F-bomb?" I offered, trying to clear it up for my mother.

On the very off chance that Mom did not get this, Riley tilted her head to one side and then slowly—and dramatically—raised her middle finger. "Fuuuzzz." She added the single eyebrow. I completely lost it.

"Oh, for God's sake!" My mother threw her hands up.

"Paige!" admonished Aunt Mo.

"Hep," said Riley, moving on to the caped devil.

"And this is . . . Jesus," I said apprehensively, worried that this was the one that would upset my mother—and Aunt Maureen—the most.

"Jay," declared Riley. "Fuz, hep, Jay." She closed the book with slow-motion flair. Aunt Maureen beamed at Riley, at how animated, how not-hurt-from-the-bathroom-incident she was.

"You don't need those words, Riley." My mother looked beyond exasperated.

"You really don't," agreed Maureen. "There are better ways to express yourself."

"You guys use these words all the time, Mom," I informed them. "And it's not just Aunt Elayne. Aunt Maureen dropped the F-bomb five times the other day when she was yelling at you guys by the elevator!"

My aunt nodded. "True. But that was an extreme circumstance—"

"What part of this isn't an extreme circumstance?" I asked.

"*Sí,*" agreed Riley. "Fuz, fuz, fuz, fuz, fuz." She was having a great time.

"I give up!" Mom declared in defeat. "Curse all you want!"

"I'm just in time, then." Elayne stood in the doorway. Despite her joke, it was obvious that she had been crying much of the night. "Can I come in?" Before anyone (my mother) could object, Riley waved her in. The last time she was here, her mother decided who came and went. My mother turned to leave; Riley gestured for her to stay.

"You look like crap," I teased Aunt Elayne.

"Nora!" snapped my mother.

"I had that one coming." Aunt Elayne grinned. I made room for her next to Riley. "Riley, I need to apologize for what happened yesterday. Paige was absolutely right and I never should have left. I was irresponsible and it was entirely my fault."

"Mine too," I added meekly. "I—I shouldn't have taken you to the bathroom. It was a dumb idea."

"Mine," said Riley. "Mine."

"True," I agreed boldly. "It was actually Riley's dumb idea." She nice-smacked me on the arm.

"Ladies!" Audra was in the doorway, tapping her foot. "Have we forgotten the visiting rules already?" There were four of us in the room, one more than the PICU allowed. Aunt Mo didn't count, so either my mom, me, or Aunt Elayne had to go. Riley jabbed a finger at my mother, her mother, and then Elayne. She gave me an open hand. Archie-speak for "stay."

"She, uh, wants me to stay," I told the others.

"Yessi," Riley confirmed.

"We'll be right outside this door," said her mother, clearly unsure. "Do NOT get out of this bed." The Sullivan sisters cleared the room together.

As soon as they were gone, Riley reached for a pen, but she couldn't quite get her fingers around it and it dropped to the floor. I put it back in her hand and gently folded her fingers around it. When I let go, the pen fell again.

"Fuz," she grunted.

Picking it up again, I realized what the problem was—the pen was too slender for her weak grip. But I had an idea. I took the pen to the bathroom and wrapped it in toilet paper until it was practically the size of a cucumber. When Riley saw it, she tilted her head the same way Archie sometimes did. I put the toilet-paper-cucumber pen in her hand and wrapped her fingers around it one more time—and then I let go. A huge smile spread across Riley's face, her hand shaking just a bit as it hovered over the family page. I resisted the urge to help steady her hand. Finally the pen settled on the page.

"You good me," she said.

"I'm good to you?"

"*Sí. Sí.*"

I didn't deserve that. I thought about hiding from her during her toughest days in the ICU, about the books I threw and kicked, and complaining about my ruined summer, and—half the time I still couldn't even bring myself to meet her gaze. But Riley hadn't witnessed any of those things. And then of course there was the fact that I was the reason she was here in the first place—only it seemed that the stroke had erased all that from her memory. She didn't remember that she shouldn't even be talking to me. I shook my head.

Riley refocused on the pen. Her grip seemed strong, but when the pen hit the page, the paper moved with her pen. Too much pressure. I held the page still as she concentrated on—and then adjusted—the point pressure. On her second attempt, the pen went through the page and tore a small hole.

"FUZ!"

"Don't give up, Ri." I smoothed over the hole

with my thumb. "Let's try a new page, where there's more room. Bigger might be easier."

She drew one shaky line. Then another. She grunted, seeming satisfied with it, but I couldn't make any sense of it. She tried again. And again.

"Wep," she said.

"I'm sorry," I said sheepishly. "I don't understand. You're spelling something?" That was a huge step, although I was suddenly nervous that despite all her hard work, I wouldn't be able to understand what she was writing. She shook her head and put the pen down. She gave up.

"Skay." But she was still looking at me.

"Want to play some more UNO?" I reached for the cards from the table, eager to put that conversation behind us.

"No. Walt." She turned to a fresh page in the notebook.

"Wait?"

"No." she said, "Walt." She turned the pages back with her good hand and stopped on:

"Wolf?" I asked. "Walt is wolf!"

"Sí, sí."

"You want to draw the wolf?"

"Sí." She kept her eyes on the sketchbook.

I eased my hand away from hers so I wouldn't be in the way. The toilet-paper-cucumber pen dropped and rolled to the end of the tray table.

"Fuh, fuz," she said.

"It's okay, we'll try again." I got the pen, and this time I wrapped my hand around Riley's and placed it on a new spot on the page.

"Walt!" She smiled. The pen was barely touching the paper, but it was enough. After a few

seconds, it started to tilt to one side as her grip loosened. I tried to hold it steady without changing what she was drawing.

"*¡Bueno* walt! *¡Bueno!*" She was happy, but her face was beginning to droop again.

"Let's take a break," I said, easing the pen out of her hand, but putting it on the tray so she could grab it easily. She was out like a light. *Beep. Beep. Beep.* I stared up at her numbers, her P SOCKS (98), her heart rate (65), and her blood pressure (110/60). She was solid, even if her memory was shaky.

Riley spent two more days in the PICU and had two more clear CT scans. Dr. Mejia was finally satisfied that the danger of the delayed hemorrhage had passed, and she had even managed to do some shuffling and put her back with Sophia in pediatrics.

Mom couldn't make Riley take the obscenities out of the notebook, but she did ask that we not use them in front of her—which Riley agreed to, but sometimes that was hard. Aunt Elayne, of course, had figured out a way around that.

She grabbed an UNO card and threw it down on Riley's tray.

"A wild card? What's that for?" I asked.

"There's your new secret F-bomb." She grinned. "Consider it a gift. I'm just going to close my eyes for a few minutes." Riley and I literally watched her fall asleep in the chair inside of one minute.

"You know they're putting your bed in the living room, right? So you don't have to use the stairs?" I babbled. "I mean, I'm sure someday you will use the stairs. . . ."

"*Sí.*" She nodded. "Know." Aunt Maureen was close by, in the hallway somewhere, and we were both under the threat of severe consequences if we moved a muscle without permission. Emergency rules were no longer in effect.

"And you know that my dad is going to build some kind of ramp so it will be easier to manage the front steps? I think he's coming this weekend so it will be ready for you."

Riley laid her hand flat on her chest and slapped herself lightly. "Me."

"Yep," I rattled on, "and a new bathroom, with bars . . . just for now . . . to help . . ."

Riley interrupted with a hand on my arm. She pointed to the ORB. I had just changed the UNO pile from red to green, and I thought she was asking me if it was her turn. Riley was in rare form back in pediatrics. She had earrings in and was wearing lip gloss! I hated the goopy feel of lip gloss, but Riley never left the house without two different shades in her bag, and by the looks of it, she had shared one of them with Sophia.

"*Sí, sí,*" I said. "It's your turn. *Verde.* Green."

"No," she said. She pointed to the picture I'd made of my dad on the communication board. She laid her hand flat on her chest and slapped herself lightly. "Me," she said. "Me." She pointed at:

And then at herself.

"You want to talk to my father?"

"No, no, no," she said. "Me. Rye. Me."

She opened and closed her hand a bunch of times then put her thumb and pointer together like she was writing with something.

"Give a note to my dad?" She reached awkwardly toward the phone and made the writing gesture.

"Fffun." Fun?

"Me fun?" I said. "Yes, Riley. You are loads of fun. For real."

Riley snorted. She grasped at a pen on the side table but only succeeded in knocking it off.

I picked it up and handed it to her. I was hoping she wasn't trying to write me a note, because she hadn't had much luck with handwriting yet. Instead she made some lines above my dad's head and then over his face a little bit.

"Are you mad at my dad for leaving? He didn't want to," I assured her. "He had to get back to work. I just told you, he's coming back to build you a ramp."

She didn't say anything. She just kept drawing. All over my dad. I listened to her scribble and Aunt Elayne snore.

Then she pointed at herself and then pointed at Scribble Dad, herself, Scribble Dad, herself, Scribble Dad. This was Scribble Dad:

You have no way of knowing who that is, but all of a sudden, I did. It was actually a pretty good version of Former Uncle Pete. "*Your* dad?"

"*Sí, sí.*"

"You want your father?"

She nodded and suddenly was crying, and trying to say something so garbled that I couldn't tell which language she was trying to use. She tried to wipe her tears, but the one hand wouldn't cooperate. It really seemed to be lagging behind the rest of her recovery—and it worried me. I grabbed a Kleenex and dabbed her cheeks as gently as I could. She pointed to her dad again and again.

"See me," she rattled.

"You thought he would come here?" I kept my voice as low as I could.

"See me," she said, looking over at Aunt Elayne and then lowering her own voice. "See me." Thoughts were ping-ponging in my brain. Why would she think he would come see her? Did he even know? If there had been a conversation about that, I definitely had not been filled in. I thought about what Mom had said in the waiting room, that Maureen hadn't spoken to Uncle Pete in two years.

Whatever had happened between Riley's parents, it must have been bad. And I still had no idea what his "problems" were. Did Riley?

"Do you know where he is?" I asked reluctantly. I had never asked her that before.

She nodded her head.

"You do?? Does . . . does your mom know?" I asked.

She shrugged.

"You miss him?" I asked. *What a stupid question,* I thought. Of course she missed him.

She nodded. "*Sí,* yes," she agreed, smiling a little, even as her eyes spilled over with tears. She sank back into the pillows, her gaze starting to drift past me. I waited for her to say something else, but it felt like she was done. I shuffled the UNO cards and dealt another round. Riley didn't pick up the cards. Instead she reached across the bed with her good arm and tapped on the phone. The phone that hadn't been used a single time since we'd been here.

"You want me to call your father?" I asked.

She shook her head. "Me," she said. "Me," and then she tapped the phone.

"*You* want to call him?" I tried not to sound as panicky as I suddenly felt.

She smacked my arm. She pointed to her mouth and then me. "Meh," she said. And then she tapped the phone.

"Yo sa," she said.

"*Yo sé,*" I repeated. *I know.* "I know? I know the phone?" I had become remarkably fluent in broken Spanish/English/Pointing. So had she.

"No, yoo *sé*."

"Yoo sa? Wait, what? You or *yo*? English or Spanish, Riley? I think you're bouncing back and forth. Start over, because I'm lost."

She pointed to *father* on the board, not *padre*.

"Okay, English," I said. "Say it in English."

"You say," she said. Then "Meh" and pointed to the phone.

"You say meh phone," I recited back to her.

"*Sí, sí, sí.*"

"Zombie Spanish Charades!" I laughed. She'd hated that joke the first time I used it, and she still hated it. She grunted a little. Grunt = mad. Snort = laugh. It was a subtle difference sometimes, but then she fished around the UNO cards until she found what she needed and threw a wild card at me. *Unmistakable.* She had just told me to go fuz myself.

"Well, same to you! This isn't easy, you know!" I threw it back at her. Aunt Elayne's head rolled in our direction. *Shoot.* I lowered my voice. "Okay, okay. I say what you are saying and showing. Me telephone. Mefone? Oh . . . my phone! My phone!"

"Yess!" Riley threw her hand up in the air.

"I have your phone," I told her, my heart quickening. "You were worried about your phone?" Worried that Aunt Maureen had it, I bet.

"Yes. *Sí.*"

"It's in your desk drawer at home. I put it there," I said. "I turned it off, too," I added quickly.

"Here," she said. "Here."

"Bring the phone here?"

"*Sí, sí,*" she said brightly. Of course she wanted her phone. She was getting better. More herself. She wanted her phone just like she wanted french fries now and her own clothes and earrings. Then it struck me. Her phone! Georgina? He had no idea where Riley was or why she seemed to have fallen off the face of the Earth! Was she worried he might be mad? Worried he might have forgotten about her?

If she was remembering Georgina, what else was she starting to remember?

"Do you remember that it's cracked?" I swallowed hard.

"No." She found the shaky lines she had drawn in the ORB. The ones I hadn't understood.

"Wep?" It was a question, I could tell from the intonation.

I saw it now. The letter Y. "Why?" I said. "Is that it?"

"Sí, sí."

"We had a fight," I explained. "You and me."

"Wep?"

I glanced over at Aunt Elayne, head now back and mouth wide open. Sound asleep. "We . . . um, had a fight. About the phone. In your room." *An awful fight,* I did not add. *You hit me,* I did not add. An awful fight about a secret boyfriend with a code name: *Georgina.* The promise I made about it and the promise I broke about it. To force her on the roller coaster. The roller coaster that landed her here. I added none of this. I wasn't going to say "Georgina" out loud, and I wasn't going to draw that ridiculous big-haired decoy.

"Wep?" Riley asked again, patting the page.

"I don't remember," I lied. Yes, I flat-out lied. My throat had gone dry. "We had a stupid little fight about something. We were tired."

She nodded, but the worst look crossed her

face, as if, all of a sudden, she was remembering, as if she was watching our fight happen all over again. Riley drew a sharp breath and her eyes got wide. Her gaze zeroed in on me. She *hissed*.

I steeled myself.

Y she demanded with her finger. With her eyes. With her shoulders.

Y she demanded with her fist.

Then she angry-pointed at me. YOU. Y .

YOU. Y .

"I'm sorry, Riley," I said. "I'm so, so sorry."

"WEP?! WEP? WEP?" *Why, why, why.*

"I don't know why!! *¡Yo no sé! ¡YO NO SÉ!*" *Why did I blackmail her? Why did I drag her on the roller coaster? Why did I make such a big deal out of a boy with a deep voice in the first place? Why?*

I reached for her hand. She snatched it away.

Beep, beep, beep, beep, beep, beep, beep.

"I just did it. It was a stupid thing! I'm just a jerk, okay! A stupid, immature jerk. I had no idea this would happen! I didn't know you would get hurt. I didn't know!!"

Both of Riley's hands were in tight fists, the left one quaking from the effort. Her chest and face had gone crimson and blotchy.

"I'm sorry, Riley. I'm so, so sorry."

She slammed both her fists against the table. The cards scattered and the table rolled. Aunt Elayne jumped up out of the chair. "What?! What?!"

I grabbed helplessly at the cards, trying to catch them. "OUT." Now she was crying. "OUT." I had managed to trigger Riley's memory—of the phone, the fight, *Georgina*, the roller coaster, the broken promise—and it was pumping through her veins, and now she couldn't stand the sight of me.

"What happened? Do you need the doctor?" Aunt Elayne was next to Riley now. "Nora, what's going on?" She looked a little frantic, like she wasn't entirely comfortable being the adult in the room.

Riley closed her eyes, then swept the ORB off the bed. It splayed open on the floor, rings popping. Plastic sheathed pages slid in every direction. She was done talking.

"¿Riley, está bien?" called Sophia. Not only was she wide awake, she was up out of bed and standing at the end of the curtain. *Are you okay?*

"No," Riley whimpered. *"No bien."*

Sophia went to Riley's bedside, sat down in my chair, and spoke to Riley in quiet Spanish while my aunt looked on. Riley answered her, but I couldn't understand them. Sophia glared at me so hard I shrank away until my back was up against the wall. She listened to Riley for another full minute before she turned her attention back to me.

"What did you do?" she seethed.

You have no idea.

Aunt Elayne excused me with a jerk of her head toward the door. I took off.

No sign of Jack in the PICU family room. Where the hell was he these days? I did two laps on the PICU floor before Monica stopped me in the hallway. I immediately felt better when I saw her.

"Do you need something for the binder, Nora?"

"I'm looking for Colin's room."

"Who?" Her smile disappeared.

"I know I'm not supposed to invade anyone's

privacy, and I'm really sorry, but I'm trying to find Colin's room so I can find Jack. You know, his brother." I really *didn't* want to invade anybody's privacy, but I really needed to talk to Jack. This wasn't a silly triangle problem. Riley remembered all of it and she hated me now.

"Colin isn't here, Nora. He hasn't been for a while."

"Colin went home?" No wonder I couldn't find Jack! Although I was a little hurt that he hadn't said good-bye or at least found me to tell me the good news.

Monica bit her lip, as if deciding something. Then she took my arm and walked me into an empty room, sliding the glass door closed.

"Nora. Colin died a few weeks ago. I'm sorry. I thought you knew."

"That's impossible! That doesn't make any sense. . . ." I had *seen* Jack. He even named the fish with Jeremy. I was right there and Jack was his usual self!

Monica looked pained. "Jack . . . still comes to the hospital. He spent an awful lot of time here; and he's . . . comfortable here. Sometimes he comes here specifically to talk with me, and sometimes he just likes to be here."

"What?" I sat in one of the visitor chairs. "But . . . why wouldn't he tell me? We had a million conversations—why wouldn't he tell me that? Why would he . . . why would he pretend that his brother was still alive?" Yes, that was by far the dumbest thing I had said since I'd been here. Why wouldn't he pretend that his brother was still alive? Wouldn't anybody if they could? Monica pulled up a chair and sat next to me. She didn't rush in to fill the silence. Even when it went on for five minutes. "He didn't want to say it out loud, did he?" I finally asked.

"Maybe."

"Are you helping him? When he comes?"

"I think so. I hope so." She smiled a little, finally.

"If . . . if I see him, should I tell him that I know? No, right? That would make it harder for him . . . wouldn't it? What should I do?" I had the sudden, terrible thought that the room we were sitting in now might have been Colin's room. What would Jack want me to do? "Maybe I should just talk normally, right? We mostly talked about fish . . . and doughnuts . . . and Fisher-Price people. He really . . . helped me."

"Did you need him for something specific today? Anything I can help you with?"

I wanted to tell her about Riley, about what I had done that was even worse than putting her on that roller coaster—I tried to cover it up. Even as she struggled to get back her words and her memories, I *hid* some of them from her. I couldn't confess that to Monica. I wasn't sure I would have been able to confess it to Jack.

"No," I finally answered, looking at her. "I'm okay." She prolonged-eye-contacted me. Reading me. Waiting for more, just in case. But I was done. When I felt my eyes sting with tears, I looked down at the floor.

"You can sit here as long as you need to, Nora. I know it's a lot to take in." Still watching my face. Still waiting for a response.

"Uh-huh" was all I could muster.

Monica left, and I moved to the window. My legs weren't frozen this time, my brain wasn't frozen, but something was, some part of me was locked in place, not wanting to know. Not wanting to let go of the idea that even though Jack's brother had cancer, and even though Colin was in intensive care, that he would just continue being sick, being here, being *alive* here.

Please don't let it have been a Code Blue; the running, the ANNOUNCEMENT. The awful thought that Jack might have heard his brother's room called on a Code Blue announcement while he made himself a cup of coffee or, even worse, been pulled out of the cube while doctors and nurses rushed past him, settled on me like a shadow. Of course he came back here, where else could you possibly go where you could surround yourself with people who wouldn't shirk away from cancer; who could handle knowing that; be okay with not only knowing it but also knowing all the hardest moments it handed to you. Where they encouraged you to sit as long as you needed to, and watched you and tried to comfort you, and where you could actually help people by being kind to their children and siblings and cousins who invariably wound up in the family room by themselves with the fish and coffee and doughnuts. But where, maybe, just maybe, you worried that telling might scare them because if they knew that your brother died there, then their person might die there too.

And maybe you just didn't want to be the floating fish in the tank in the PICU family room.

DAY 13½

I don't know how long I sat in that empty cube. Monica was true to her word and never bothered me or hurried me along. I finally left when I realized that Jack might actually spot me in there— and I had no idea how I'd handle that. Worse, if he saw me in a cube by myself, he would try to cheer me up, and I knew it would be too much and I'd blurt everything out. So I used the stairwell, the bathroom, even the lobby and the nursery to avoid Jack, avoid Riley, and avoid every conversation I didn't know how to have. And I managed to do just that, until I got in the car.

"Elayne said Riley was upset today." Aunt Mo was turned halfway around in the front passenger seat. "Do you know anything about that?" Shoot. How much had Aunt Elayne told her?

"Yeah, she seemed a little . . . agitated," I answered. "Agitated" was the word Mom and Aunt Mo used whenever Riley struggled with something. Not upset or angry, but "agitated." Like a washing machine.

"I hope she didn't upset you," Aunt Mo continued. I couldn't tell if Aunt Elayne had just misinterpreted what had happened between Riley and me or if she knew *exactly* what happened and chose to leave out the details for Aunt Mo. How long had she really been asleep anyway?

"Not really," I mumbled.

"I know it's hard when she's . . . not herself." Not herself? Which self were we talking about? The secret-boyfriend-push-you-to-the-floor self (which Aunt Mo knew nothing about)? Or just the 100 percent big-smile-walking-talking-and-using-the-bathroom-by-herself self?

"No, it's okay." I smiled nervously. "I understand." *I understand a lot more than you do,* I thought.

* * *

Finally, at home, I kicked off my sneakers and threw my backpack down on the floor of Riley's room. More than anything, I wanted a door to shut. I took out my notebook and looked down at the moronic words I had drawn when I was feeling sorry for myself because Jack was too busy for me. Busy trying to make Jeremy feel better in the PICU family room. Jack keeping this, what, eight-year-old boy company and naming fish with him, like he had done with me.

Harry Potter   skateboarding

doughnuts

Had I really wanted to give Riley words? Or had I just been uncomfortable with the hospital words? *Pain. Medicine. Nurse. Bedpan.* Jack's words too:

T-cells. Cancer. Leukemia. No, he hadn't told me about Colin . . . but how could I not have known? I hadn't known because I was too busy talking about myself, my triangles, my cousin, my running. I hadn't really listened, had I? Yes, Monica's prolonged looks were annoying sometimes, but they were invitations. Invitations to talk, if you wanted to. To say more. To explain. To take a minute and feel something instead of spraying words out into the air. I had changed the subject often and quickly with Jack, whenever things got slightly uncomfortable. Jack, who wore the same clothes for two or three days in row. Jack, never with family in the family room. Jack, who shifted uncomfortably when I mentioned Colin in the triangle game. Who left abruptly when I had written I wanted to meet his brother. Why would Jack tell me the hardest thing in the world when I hadn't really been listening to anything? Jack was lost and went to the only place he could find that felt familiar. I still had no idea what I was going to do when, and if, I saw him again before we would leave the hospital for good. Jack had been on my team, but I wasn't so sure I had been on his—and he desperately needed one.

And had I really listened to Riley? How long had she been hiding this boyfriend, and how long had I not really been paying attention? I rummaged around through her desk until I found her phone, exactly where I had thrown it. The battery was dead now. I dug deeper until I found the charger.

It took an hour, but finally the bar was fully lit. You know how they tell you never to use your birthday for a password? That was exactly what Riley did, and so I got in on the first try. The phone lit up like crazy. I quickly made sure the ringer was off, too. Her voice mail was full and there were more text messages than I could count. I'm not going to lie and say I didn't read them, because I did. Some of them, anyway. Most of them were from the first few days after the stroke. It seemed like after that, her friends had heard what happened and knew their texts weren't going to be answered. Only one person had kept texting and calling.

 GEORGINA: WHERE DID U GO?

I'm in the hospital, I wanted to say.

HELLO?

I MISS YOU.

ARE YOU ANGRY?

I am very angry, I wanted to say.

I NEED TO TALK TO YOU.

I can't talk right now because I've had a stroke,
I wanted to say.

I wanted to say a lot. I laced up my sneakers
and ran downstairs, and out the back door, Archie
in his now usual spot at my side. I left the phone,
hidden under the bed so Aunt Maureen wouldn't
come across it.

"What are you up to?" Aunt Maureen called
after me from the window.

"Just stretching my legs!" I answered. "And
Archie's!"

"Thanks, Nora!" She was so happy and cheerful these last two days, getting everything ready for
Riley to come home. I wanted to take care of *one*
thing for her.

I thought about "Georgina" as I stretched on the
deck. I didn't know anything about who he was,
or where he lived, or whether he would even care

about Riley. I did one lap around the yard to get my brain going. But I did know he should have left my thirteen-year-old cousin Riley alone. *He* was going to listen to *me*. Another lap around the yard. It was the one thing I should have done weeks ago that I actually had a second chance to get right.

My heart was not pumping fast enough. I touched the fence and then sprinted to the other side. I imagined our conversation as my legs pounded.

Hi, you don't know me, but you are in big trouble.

Touched the fence and sprinted back.

Who is this?

None of your business.

Touched the fence and sprinted back.

Where is Riley? Who is this?

Nora. Nora Reeves. I am her cousin, and you need to know what you did.

Touched the fence and sprinted back.

Where is Riley?

Riley had a stroke because of you. I won't tell you where because you don't belong anywhere near her. You ruined her life, you ruined her mother's life, and you ruined mine. I just thought you should know.

Touched the fence. And walked off the stitch in my side. Dripping with sweat, I took the inside stairs two at a time and hopped into the shower. I used Riley's coconut shampoo and slowly turned off the hot water until it was as cold as I could stand it. I wasn't sure if it was having a plan, or fixing a mistake, but I felt better than I had in a while, which was weird because I also knew Riley hated me now. Maybe I just felt better because I had nothing to lose.

The phone was fully charged and in my backpack, and I fell fast asleep with Archie curled next to me, his nose nestled in my coconut hair.

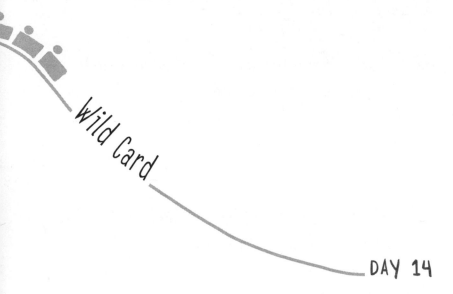

When I woke up the next morning, I took Archie out for a quick run around the block. Have I mentioned he was huge? He didn't need a walk, he needed to run, poor boy. When we had finished one lap around the block, Archie was still bounding and loving every minute. I took him around two more times.

By the time I got back, Mom and Aunt Maureen were dressed and ready to go. Now all I had to do was get out, way out, of earshot of my family. As we entered the hospital, I announced that I was taking the stairs.

"Sure." Mom left without giving me a second thought. As soon as the elevator doors closed, I swung around and headed back outside. Were my hands shaking as I took Riley's phone out of my backpack? Yes, they were. I could barely thumb through the address book.

 GEORGINA

I paced back and forth, practicing my talk into the phone, even though I hadn't even dialed yet. No one paid any attention to me. I rehearsed my speech three times as people came and went out of the hospital. Walked in. Walked out. Some ran.

I took one last big breath.

 GEORGINA

I hit dial.

Ring, ring, ring. I had just about lost my nerve— would I leave a message? I hadn't considered that! My stomach knots were crawling up my throat, when I heard a man's voice. *The* man.

"Riley? Where have you been?"

I couldn't respond.

"Riley?" the man said again. "What's going on? Where have you been?" He was angry.

"This isn't Riley," I said, suddenly unsure of

myself. I was pacing again. My voice had gone shaky, and the words I'd practiced wouldn't come out of my mouth.

"Who is this? I've been trying to reach Riley for weeks! What happened? Where is she?" He didn't sound angry anymore. He sounded worried— almost panicked. "Who is this? Is Riley with you?"

"Yes. No. Kind of . . ." I stopped pacing. I was blowing this, big-time. I had to get it together. "I know your fake girl code name: Georgina!" I blurted out.

"What's happened to Riley? Where is she? Let me talk to her."

I never imagined that the jerk would sound so scared. It threw me. "Riley had a stroke. It's *your* fault. You gave Riley a stroke!"

"Is this a joke? This isn't funny. I don't know who you are, but you'd better put Riley on the phone."

"She never wants to see you again, and you will be in big trouble if you ever call her or come near her. We will have you arrested if you come anywhere near her. I mean it. HAVE YOU ARRESTED! ARE YOU LISTENING TO ME?? YOU

WILL BE HANDCUFFED, YOU STUPID F-BOMB F-BOMBING[44] JERK!" Then "Georgina" began to shout right over me.

"I'm going to say this one time, so you listen good. My name is Peter McMorrow, and I am Riley's father. If you don't put my daughter on the phone in the next five seconds, *you* are going to be in more trouble than you've ever imagined. Do you understand me? PUT MY DAUGHTER ON THE PHONE THIS INSTANT!"

Wait. What? WHAT? Who? OMG. OMG. Everything I had been thinking and feeling about Riley's "boyfriend" shattered into pieces. Riley's boyfriend . . . wasn't a boyfriend. Georgina was her *father*. HER FATHER. And I had just ambushed Uncle Pete—her father—with terrible, awful news. I couldn't even say my name. *Uncle Pete?* I felt like my brain was buzzing with static, beginning to shut down. And then I realized that he was crying. Uncle Pete was crying.

"How did this . . . how did this happen to her?" he finally choked out. "Oh my God. Oh my . . ."

---

[44] I said the real words. Screamed them.

Words clattered in my head. *Hospital, stroke, roller coaster, emergency, bedpan, P-SOCKS, AFib.* I hung up. For an instant, I couldn't even think. I could barely remember what I had been trying to do in the first place. *RING, RING, RING.*

 GEORGINA

I stared at the phone. I had no idea what to do. Answer? Don't answer? *RING, RING, RING.*

 GEORGINA

I let it ring. Ahead of me, across six lanes of traffic, I saw the Abraham Lincoln face on that sign. I understood that. I recognized that. I ran toward it.

Cars began honking and people began screaming at me. I was in the middle of the street. I was shaking. DON'T WALK. DON'T WALK. DON'T WALK. What did I do? Riley's father? Uncle Pete? Georgina? The roller coaster? The stroke? DON'T WALK. Solid this time. I didn't. I stood. I kept my eyes on Abraham Lincoln's face hanging off the streetlamp. DON'T TALK. DON'T WALK. DON'T TALK. I turned my head just in time to see a car coming straight at me. Brakes squealed. STOP

STOP STOP. I was trapped in between lanes, in between cars. *RING, RING, RING.* "Move!" "Idiot!" "You trying to get killed?" Somebody was running toward me, between the cars, hands thrown up and wide—stopping traffic. "Get out of the way!" I couldn't remember how I got where I was. I was too scared to go back. *BEEEEEP. BEEEEEEP. BEEEEEEEPP.* The angry driver in the closest car gave up and drove around me. Another followed. A car door opened. Someone was yelling. WAIT, WAIT, WAIT. There was no place for me to go. Too many cars. Then somebody was next to me, holding my hand. Someone I didn't know. "Honey, are you okay?" The sign turned. WALK. WALK. WALK. I didn't walk. I couldn't walk. My whole body— and my brain—shook, and I just couldn't find my brain or my words or my feet. Oh no. *Riley.* This is *you. This* is what I did to you. Words and sounds and people and thoughts and feelings and memories shattered, cracked, and spilled everywhere around you—all unreachable. My knees buckled. *RING, RING, RING.*

"Come on. Come on, sweetheart." A girl was grabbing at my arms, lifting me, almost carrying me. "Out of the street. It's okay. You're okay." She walked me back to the sidewalk. I leaned into her the entire way. I said nothing. Thought nothing. The horns stopped. I finally felt my feet in my shoes again. *RING, RING, RING.* I felt the phone in my hand. "Are you lost? Are you by yourself? Where are your parents?" *RING, RING, RING.*

I gestured toward the hospital. The girl walked me to the front entrance and sat me down on a bench. She looked about eighteen or nineteen years old. She had super-short blond hair, lightning bolt-earrings, and her Doctor Who T-shirt was tied in a knot. "Can I call someone for you?" *RING, RING, RING.* I finally pressed the ignore button.

"Nobody, thanks. I'm okay." I was still shaking, but my head was beginning to clear. "Really, I'm okay. I just got . . . confused." She didn't look convinced. "I thought I could make it across the street and I just got scared. Thank you. Thank you for helping me." One of Riley's nurses walked past and waved at me. "Hi, Nora!"

"You sure you're okay? I can walk you inside if you want."

"I'm okay. You're very nice. Thank you." I

shoved my hands under my legs to calm them down. It helped to feel my own body. The girl stood up. "You sure now?"

"Yes." I nodded. "I'm sure."

"All right then, girl. You be careful. Wait for the light next time."

"I will," I promised. "Thanks again," I called after her. I watched her walk away toward the parking lot. She turned back around one more time. To be sure.

I took a few deep breaths, head down, eyes on my feet. I had to call Uncle Pete back. But I had to talk to Riley first. If only she wanted to talk to me.

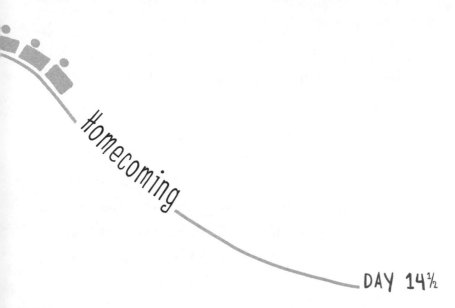

DAY 14½

My legs were too shaky for the stairs. In the elevator, I hit the button for ten—the PICU—instead of eight, where Riley was now. I wanted to sit in the family room, eat a doughnut, wait for Monica, and then spill my guts. To finally take her up on her invitation to listen. But the doors opened and there was no one. No Jack. No Monica. Just the happy blue river on the floor and the usual buzz of activity. I didn't get out.

"Hey! There you are!" There was a crowd outside Riley's room. Aunt Maureen was verging on giddy. "Great news! It's official! Riley's coming home on Monday!!" She proceeded to tell me every detail.

"We don't think she's quite ready for school, but there's a good chance she'll be able to go back after Christmas break—after some rehabilitation, of course!" I gave my brightest smile and was genuinely, deeply happy and relieved for Aunt Maureen—and for Riley. "Go on in there and give her a big going-home hug!!" Right. Riley would love that. But Aunt Mo was on a roll, and she grabbed me and pulled me into the room with her.

"Congratulations, Riley," I said, my bright smile still shining.

Riley gave me forced half smile but didn't answer me.

"Riley, don't be rude. Nora is standing right here and she's talking to you." Aunt Mo was back to treating Riley like 100 percent Riley. Before she could take it any further, my mother called Aunt Maureen into the hallway. Aunt Elayne was busy with the *New York Times* and had barely said a word either. She knew something was up with Riley and me, but she had decided to stay out of it.

Clearly, Riley didn't want me there any more than I wanted to be there. No tomato soupin'. She definitely did not want to talk to me, but I needed to talk to her . . . about her father. Tell her what happened. That I'd been wrong, and now I knew the truth. But I wanted to do it privately. Because I was not keeping it all to myself this time. If Riley didn't tell her mother, then I felt like I had to do it. It was pretty clear that she was afraid of Aunt Maureen finding out. Otherwise, why the code name? Why the terror on her face when her mother grabbed the phone during our fight? If she was hiding her relationship with her father, there had to be a reason. I wanted to understand what was really happening.

I avoided my regular seat next to Riley and stood against the wall. Sophia wasn't in her bed, so the curtain was pulled back and I could stare out the window, as if something interesting was going on outside. But I could sense Riley's eyes on me.

"Excited to go home?" I asked her. She shrugged and closed her eyes. Didn't want to talk to me, and now didn't want to look at me.

But now Aunt Elayne wanted help with her crossword puzzle. "Five-letter word, starts with *B*. An emblem that signifies your status. Hmmm . . ."

"Um, don't know," I muttered.[45]

"You're not much help, are you?" she asked.

"No," Riley blurted out. "No help."

Aunt Elayne chuckled, thinking Riley was making a joke. "Maybe you can help me with this instead of Nora! I'm sure it would be a good brain exercise for you." She scooted her chair toward the head of the bed so Riley could see the puzzle. She didn't seem to notice when Riley shot me a dirty look before she turned her attention to the newspaper. How was I going to get Aunt Elayne out of the room?

I went right for the truth. "I really need to talk to Riley about something. Could you . . . would you mind leaving us alone for just one minute?" I peeked over at Riley, but she was staring down at the crossword puzzle she was holding a little too close to her face. Avoiding me.

"Your mother will kill me." Aunt Elayne hesitated, but something in my voice or in my face convinced her. She stood up. "I'll be right out in the hall. . . ."

---

[45] So you don't drive yourself crazy . . . the answer is "badge."

"No!" Riley cried out. "Not you!" She sat straight up and glared at me. Aunt Elayne, to her credit, didn't flinch. She shifted her eyes from me to Riley. "Not you," Riley went on. "Not you."

Riley grabbed Aunt Elayne's pen right out of her hand and flipped (very quickly, I might add) through the ORB. She held the pen in her fist like a little kid and began scratching at something. Then turned the book around angrily, so I could see.

"You out! You OUT!" she barked.

Aunt Elayne dropped the newspaper on the bed. "What the . . . ? Riley? Calm down!"

"Fine," I spat out, snatching the newspaper. "Have it your way, Riley. I don't even care anymore!" I threw the newspaper *in her face*. I didn't care if it hurt, either.

"Nora!" Aunt Elayne cried.

"No!" Riley grabbed me by the arm, but I yanked it away. Aunt Elayne stepped in between us, like Riley was the one she had to protect.

"I shouldn't have blackmailed you, but *you* shouldn't have lied! *You* should have told me the truth about Georgina!" I jabbed my finger at her wildly.

"Georgina?" said Elayne. "Who the hell is Georgina?"

"I just called him, and I told him what happened to you!"

Riley's mouth fell open.

"I was trying to HELP!"

Elayne locked eyes with me, her arms still spread wide. Riley pushed them out of her way and swung her legs over the side of the bed. She was coming at me.

"What are you going to do? Push me again? Knock me down again? You HURT ME when you did that! You *hurt* me!" I had no idea all this anger was waiting inside of me. I felt the phone in my pocket and launched it at her too, missing her by a mile, but satisfied that it ricocheted off the headboard and clattered onto the floor. "Here! Here's your precious phone! I know it's more important to you than anything!"

Riley picked up the ORB with her bad hand and threw it at me. It grazed my shoulder and then bounced off the chair. Riley struggled to stand up and lurched toward me. "NO, NO, NO!" She was screaming at the top of her lungs as my aunt tried to physically hold her down. With her attention off me, I ran out the door, past the nurses who were racing toward Riley's room. I could still hear Riley yelling, "NO, NO, NO!" as I ran down the hall to the stairs. On the ground floor, I charged past the security guard, past the gift shop, and right out the front door.

I ran toward the Cyclone.

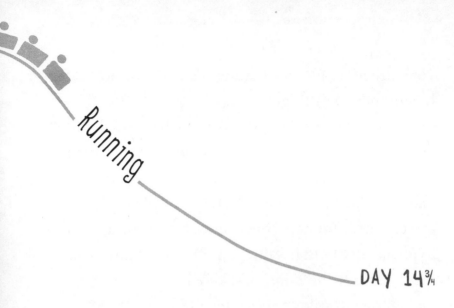

DAY 14¾

I counted my steps as I ran, listened to *my* heart-beat for a change, and found *my* breath. Feeling steadier and stronger each time my sneakers hit pavement. I wasn't afraid of what was happening back at the hospital. It was over. Riley could go home and I could go home. I ran across Sea Breeze Avenue and then Surf Avenue, under the subway and up to the boardwalk. It was the longest, flattest line I'd ever run.

It was hot and humid, and sweat was already pouring down my face. The ocean was like syrup, no roars today, no crashing waves, just halfhearted licks at the sand. I pumped my arms and ran even faster past the aquarium, past the handball courts just beyond it, games still pop-pop-popping even in the stifling heat. Then the adrenaline that had gotten me there gave out. I found an empty bench and collapsed onto it. My shirt and shorts were heavy with sweat, and I stuck to the back of the bench. I hadn't paced myself at all, and I was feeling shaky. I bent forward, heard the blood rushing into my head, and was certain I was going to vomit . . . again. Then all of it, all the beach noises—the subway, the ocean, the people, the roller coaster—folded into each other until it felt like . . . silence. Finally. I could enjoy silence again, without feeling guilty about it, or worrying about it, or feeling the anger that delivered it. It was a good quiet for a change. Old quiet. It didn't last fifteen minutes.

"Nora!"

Oh no, really? My mother was running toward me. She must have pulled an Emergency Room Run to get to me that quickly. "Nora!" Her voice was strained—she was huffing and puffing when she got to the bench.

"How did you know where I was?" I asked, jumping up, furious that my one moment was already over.

"Jack," she said, bending over, panting. "He thought . . . you might . . . take a run." I stood up and searched the boardwalk, hoping to see Jack coming toward me, but instead recognized Elayne about a block away, Aunt Maureen a half block behind her.

"All of you? Ran here?"

"We grabbed . . . a cab . . . in front of . . . the hospital," she said. "We're not . . . that crazy."

"Nora! Nora!" Elayne was sort of half running and half walking in her wedge-heeled sandals. *Interesting,* an odd part of my brain thought—my mother was a much faster runner than Elayne. The whole Sullivan Triangle was huffing and puffing its way toward me.

Then my regular brain kicked back in.

"Just leave me alone!" I hollered. "I'll come back when I feel like it!" I sat back down on the bench and folded my arms across my chest. "I don't want to talk to anybody! And besides, *God forbid* you leave Riley alone for a single second . . ."

My mother sat down next to me. "It's not Riley I'm worried about. It's . . . you." Her shirt was spotted with perspiration, and she was still a little out of breath.

Elayne dropped down on the other side of me and unbuckled her shoes. "Riley nearly knocked me to the floor. I'd say she's feeling pretty good." She was panting like a dog.

"Thank God you're okay." Now Aunt Maureen was standing in front of me, blocking the sun. I half expected to see Riley limping down the boardwalk next, rolling her monitor behind her. I had to look to make sure that wasn't actually happening.

"Are you okay, Maureen?" asked Aunt Elayne, frowning up at her. Aunt Maureen's face could not possibly have been more red. "You should sit down. Here, take my spot. You look like you're going to pass out!"

"I'm . . . fine." Aunt Maureen bent over with her hands on her knees. "Leave . . . us . . . alone . . . guys," she said to her sisters. Her eyes were bloodshot. She sat down and wiped the sweat off her face with the back of her hand. She was still breathing a bit too hard. I worried about her P-SOCKS, and her heart rate must have been through the roof. It didn't feel like the time to point out her own risk for a heart attack.

I wasn't sure if I wanted to be alone with Aunt Maureen. But Elayne nodded to my mom and they walked away, half holding each other up. There was an empty bench not far away, but they didn't sit. Mom started to sit down at the next one after that, but Aunt Elayne—now barefoot!—tugged her forearm and forced her farther down the board-walk, back toward the hospital.

I kept my eyes on an old woman who was throwing bread to the seagulls. The boardwalk was quiet today. Must have been the humidity. I liked it that way.

"You want to tell me about Georgina?"

I froze. "What??" Oh no. Aunt Elayne must have already told her about the conversation.

"I asked Riley, but she wouldn't answer me," she added. "If it's a big enough deal that Elayne had to pin Riley down to the bed and you had to run away, I think it's something I need to know about."

"Well, Georgina . . . is . . ." This was the do-over I wanted, wasn't it? To tell Riley's mother some-thing she didn't know, but should? Riley hated me anyway, right? And, yes, Aunt Maureen needed to know. "Um, well . . . I didn't know this until today, but, um, Georgina is Uncle Pete."

"Hang on, you lost me already. I don't understand. . . ."

"In Riley's phone . . . That's what he's called in Riley's phone. . . . Riley talks to her dad. And, well, I spoke to him too. Today. This morning. I told him Riley had a stroke."

"What?" The tone of her voice flipped like a switch. Panic rose in my chest. I looked down the boardwalk, hoping my mom and Elayne had changed their minds and were coming back for us. But there was no help in sight. "I didn't know it was him. I thought I was calling Riley's boyfriend, and then I didn't know who it was and then when he told me who he actually was . . . it was too late. . . ."

"Wait, what? Boyfriend? Nora, what are you talking about?" Aunt Maureen's nostrils flared. She opened her mouth as if say something more but seemed to think better of it, because instead she popped up and bolted to the railing. I waited. She took a giant breath and blew it out slowly, then turned back to me. "Okay. Okay . . . one thing at a time, right? One thing at a time . . ." She wasn't actually talking to me, she was talking to herself, I think? I didn't know. She ran her hands through her hair until it was almost as big as Aunt Elayne's. She looked at me one last time. Then she just walked away. And just kept walking. Beyond her, my mom and Aunt Elayne were practically specks. The wind was picking up and Aunt Maureen's hair whipped around her head. She tried to hold it down, but the wind took it right back up. Alone, walking away, she reminded me of Riley walking away from the Cyclone because she had been afraid. I bit my lip so hard it hurt.

I stood up, took a deep breath myself, and jogged after my aunt. She turned around, as if she was expecting me, and reached for my hand.

"I should have called her father," she said, as if we'd just been in the middle of a normal conversation seconds ago. "That was my responsibility, but I just had all that I could take, you know? I didn't . . . I didn't want to deal with him, too." Her eyes brimmed with tears. "He's had some problems"— she hesitated—"with drugs. Well, lots of problems. For a long time. I didn't want Riley to know. I didn't want to upset her." Aunt Maureen took a step back from me. "What did you say to him?"

I was afraid to tell her how badly I had messed up that phone call. But it was more than the phone call I was hiding.

"I shouted and I cursed and I told him it was his fault. But I didn't know I was talking to him—Uncle Pete," I went on. "I thought Riley had a boyfriend. An older boyfriend . . ." A funny look crossed my aunt's face, but it passed.

"How long have they been in touch?" she asked, blinking rapidly.

"I don't know," I answered. "I really don't. But why *can't* she talk to him? He's her father." My aunt stiffened. She looked past me and out to the beach. The waves were picking up and a light rain began to fall. The lifeguards put on their big sweatshirts and pulled their stands back from the surf.

"Drugs change people, Nora. And they changed him. Made him a different person. Unpredictable. Unreliable. Scary sometimes. He tried at first to stay in touch, show up for Riley. But then he just stopped."

"Riley doesn't know about his . . . problems?"

317

"I told her about some of it . . . but not all of it. Enough for her to understand that he loved her, but we might not see him again."

Sadness began to seep into me. For Aunt Maureen. For Riley. Even for Uncle Pete. I couldn't imagine hearing that about my father. I wondered why she'd never told me. And I realized . . . I realized now why she got on the roller coaster: she wasn't afraid of Aunt Maureen being angry, she was afraid of losing her father again.

"The thing is . . ." My eyes filled with tears. "That's how I got her on the roller coaster." The tears spilled over as the words came out. "I blackmailed her. I thought she was hiding a boyfriend from you. I didn't know it was her dad. I threatened to tell you about him, the boyfriend, I mean, if she didn't get on the Cyclone with me. She didn't *want* to get on the roller coaster. She was too scared. I *made* her go." The floodgates opened. "I didn't know, Aunt Maureen, I didn't know she had a heart problem!"

Aunt Maureen looked stricken. The wind rattled through my wet clothes. I began to shiver.

"No, no, sweetheart." She wrapped her arms

around me. "This is *not* your fault." She stepped back, so I could see her face. She was crying with me. "Riley was going to have a stroke whether she went on that roller coaster or not. Her heart wasn't working right and the clot was going to break loose sooner or later. I know that's a tough thing to think about, but it's true. In fact, if she had had the stroke in her sleep, we wouldn't have known it for hours, and things could be a lot worse than they are right now. A lot worse. So actually, it might have been the best bad thing that could have happened."

"Does Riley know that?" A trio of seagulls squawked and screeched, competing for the last few scraps of bread on the ground.

"I don't know, Nora." She had her eyes on the seagulls now too. "If you blame yourself, maybe Riley blames you too." The trio strutted toward us, expecting bread. Aunt Maureen flapped her hands and shooed them off. They screeched in complaint. Greedy birds.

"But we were okay, you know?" I was pleading my case. "We played UNO and we had the wolves and I helped her and we laughed and it seemed like we were okay!"

"Look at it this way—maybe now she's strong enough to be angry. That's a good thing."

"So she's going to get better and better and then turn around and be mad at me all over again?"

"Maybe," my aunt said honestly.

"So what do I do now?" I asked, eyeing the sky, watching the darker clouds roll in.

"Exactly what you're doing," she said. "Stick around. Play UNO. Read to her. Give her words. Drop her on the bathroom floor . . ."

"Aunt Maureen!!"

She swatted my arm. "I'm just teasing. It was actually kind of *good* that you took her to the bathroom. I was too scared to do it. She'd asked me to take her, but I was afraid. . . ." She shook her head like she was disappointed in herself.

"Afraid of what?"

"Well . . . afraid she would fall."

"But she did!"

"Yes, she did. And then she was okay. It was an important step for her to take—to be independent and feel like herself again—and you took it with her. That's a big thing, sweetheart."

"I was out-of-my-mind scared," I admitted,

remembering the crash and the noise and the diaper. Remembering how I thought I had hurt her . . .
again. "Um, well, there is one more thing. . . ."

Aunt Mo stopped walking and hung her head
dramatically. "Go ahead."

"Well, I . . . um . . . threw Riley's phone at her.
I was going to give it to her today and then I got
so upset, and my adrenaline was pumping, and
then . . . well . . . I just sorta hurled it at her."

"Wow, she is *really* gonna be mad at you now,"
she said. "You didn't hurt her, did you?"

"No, I missed," I said, feeling ridiculous. "But,
I may have also broken it. It kinda bounced off
Riley's headboard?" The rain continued, and we
walked faster toward the hospital. "I know you
must be really mad. . . ."

"About a phone?" She gave me a *really?* look.

"You were so mad when we cracked it a few
weeks ago!"

"That was then. This is . . . now." We were
coming up on Third Street, but even the handball
courts were almost deserted—just a few stragglers,
packing up their folding chairs. They didn't seem
to mind the rain.

"Yeah, now is . . . now." The wind was picking up and it made me even colder. I leaned in closer to her to warm up. "Do you think he'll come see her? Riley really wants him to."

"I'll talk to him," she promised. "And then I'll talk to Riley. I don't know if he's in any shape to come see her," she added. Then she stopped and looked around. "I don't really know where we are."

"I do," I said. "We're just past the handball courts, and we turn left at the onion smell. I know the way."

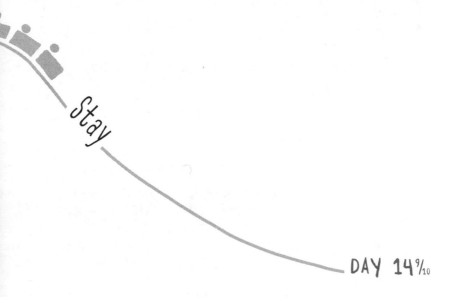

DAY 14 %10

Aunt Maureen let me go up to see Riley on my own. Sand squished and scratched in my sneakers. Sophia was in her bed, the curtain open, talking quietly to Riley in Spanish. She stopped when I came in. Someone had picked up the ORB and put it back on Riley's tray table.

"Hey," I said to Riley.

"Hey." She didn't look up.

I took the chair closest to the door. And then I went for it, Sophia there or not. "I need to talk to you about your father," I said. "I'm upset. . . . I'm upset that you lied about him. I know it might not seem as bad as a secret boyfriend, but I was really worried about you. Because I didn't know it wasn't a boyfriend who was way too old and dangerous! You didn't tell me!"

Riley didn't say anything.

"I called your father," I admitted. "I thought I was calling your boyfriend—to tell him off—but it was your dad . . . and I was so surprised . . . and I really blew it."

Riley was looking at me now, waiting for more. Anxious.

"He's been worried about you. Trying to reach you." I didn't tell her that he cried, because I didn't want *her* to worry about *him*, and I knew she would. That wasn't the toughest part, though. I steeled myself for the hardest part, hearing Marisol's voice in a hard run, *Stay with me here.*

"I told your mom, too." I expected a stronger reaction, but she barely blinked. I think she was relieved, at least a little bit. She still wouldn't look at me, but she'd been nodding slowly here and there, so I knew she was listening.

I stopped talking and she stopped nodding and we were in that terrible quiet place, until, in perfect English, Riley said softly, "Come here?" She swallowed hard.

"Your dad? I don't know." I paused. I decided it wasn't for me to explain. "You should probably talk to your mom about it." Riley didn't reply. "I'm sorry I threw your phone."

She shrugged. I guess Aunt Maureen wasn't the only one who didn't think the phone was so important anymore.

"Mad you."

"I know. You're mad that I gave you a stroke. I . . . understand that. And you have every right." I said it. I finally said. It. Even though Aunt Maureen told me that wasn't true, it was still true to Riley.

"No."

What? No? What did she mean, no? Then what was she mad about?

"Meh tell you." She tugged the notebook toward her, turned the page to the family page, and then flipped the pages, going back and forth, like she was planning ahead what she wanted to say.

"Do you want help?" I reached for it. "I'm going to make you index cards with the words, so you don't have to turn the pages—it will be easier. You can line them up in a row . . . build a whole sentence instead of flipping back and forth." I had gotten the idea yesterday, in fact, but hadn't wanted to help her then.

"No, is okay." She began:

Riley

I hadn't seen that one before. It was on Sophia's page. "Boo? Like a ghost?" I asked.

"Afraid," Sophia said from her bed.

"You're afraid of me?" I flashed back to the moment I had thrown the newspaper in her face and then the phone.

"No." She shook her head. She slid her hand over the page, like she was wiping it clean.

"Okay, starting over," I said.

She nodded and pointed again.

"Riley afraid," I repeated.

"Yes."

Her hands were moving a mile a minute—she was struggling to find one specific word in a brain that held a jumble of them. Her frustration was growing—and her heart rate was going up with it.

"I'm sorry, Riley. . . . I don't know . . ."

She grabbed the marker and turned the page. I held the corners down as she drew:

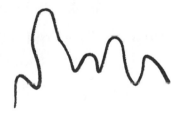

"Letters? Is that script? Are you trying to write something or draw something? Is it Spanish?" I was spitting out my questions too fast. *Slow down,* I told myself. *Wait for Riley.* Listen *to Riley.*

She tapped her fingers on the table, deep in thought.

"Can I help?" Sophia's voice was thin. She was struggling to get up. She had an oxygen tube—a cannula—running under her nostrils today. I hadn't seen that before. That was new. Or had I just not noticed it? I stood in front of her, made sure Sophia's feet were wide apart, and then helped pull her up. She was taller than me, but she felt small in my arms. She held on to my shoulders as I lowered her into her visitor's chair and then pushed her closer to Riley. Her oxygen tubes were almost taut, so I repositioned her chair.

"*¿Está bien?*" asked Riley, looking at the tubes.

"*Sí, gracias,*" said Sophia. She looked down at the loops Riley had drawn, skipping past Riley's obvious worry about her cannula. "Letters? School?" guessed Sophia. "Are you afraid to go back to school?" That hadn't occurred to me at all.

"No."

What could Riley be afraid of? *Oh. Now I see it.*

And I knew. I could say it for her, but she wanted to say it herself. It was her story. Not mine. I knew the word she needed, and it wasn't in the note-book. It was in my backpack. I rushed to it and dug around. It was ripped and wrinkled and trapped by Abraham Lincoln. The page I had ripped out of her sketchbook when I saw it for the first time in the PICU family room:

Riley seemed mesmerized by it. Did she remember drawing it?

"You are afraid of the roller coaster?" asked Sophia.

"Yes."

And then Riley made the sign of the cross.

"*Really* afraid," added Sophia, smiling. She really did understand Riley.

"¡Sí!"

"Sí." Then she pointed at me—a different kind of point, like her different silences and her different grunts. She pointed an angry finger. Hands can be just as angry as voices—and silence. You just learn to know the difference.

Nora

"Riley is afraid of the roller coaster. Nora . . . ," recited Sophia.

"Not," Riley said clearly and slowly, a deliberate "not."

She was deep in thought, raising and then lowering her hands. She couldn't find a word or a way to explain it.

She was crying now.

"Not . . . care," I said for her. "I didn't care." I was upset now too. "She told me so many times," I choked out. "So many times . . ."

"I don't get it," Sophia said. "When?" Riley pointed at me, asking for help, telling me it was

my turn. She needed me to string it together, to say it out loud for her. For me to hear.

"The night before we went to the amusement park, Riley and I had a fight—" Riley put her hand up and stopped me. I guess she didn't want to share that part—it was private to her—and it was really about her father. Sophia didn't need the details. She didn't need to know about Code Name Georgina. She didn't need to know that Riley tried to get out of the line and I blackmailed her. She didn't need to know that riding the roller coaster was the last thing she did before she had a stroke. The details didn't matter to her, or to Riley, or to me anymore either. It wasn't about the phone, or Georgina, or even the stroke. It was so much simpler than all that.

"Riley was afraid, but I only cared about what I wanted." Saying it out loud was awful.

"Fuz you," Riley said.

"I know." Tears were forming again. "You were so scared. . . . I didn't listen to you. I'm so, so sorry." And even though I knew it was coming and even though I knew I deserved it for being so selfish and so uncaring, when Riley exploded,

when it actually hit me, it was almost too much to bear. She yelled and she cursed and her hands, her face, her eyes were so angry at me—so hurt by me. When I finally thought she was done—had said it all—I put my head down on her arm, and I cried. She pulled me closer and cried too.

We went on like that for a while, until Aunt Maureen came in from the hallway. It was her turn to talk now. She would have to find the words that Riley needed. Different words. I had no idea what they would be. But it wasn't really any of my business. If Riley wanted to tell me later, she would. And if she didn't, I would have to live with that, too. She might just share pieces of it. She might have even tried to tell me about her dad before, but I just wasn't listening the right way. She might even forget all of it tomorrow—and remember it again in a week. I helped Sophia back to bed and then left Riley and Aunt Maureen, already deep in conversation.

The PICU family room was busy. Television on, coffee brewing, fish swimming. I had mixed feelings

when I spotted Jack in his usual spot. Jeremy next to him now, looking slightly less shell-shocked. Jack looked up when I came in and waved excitedly. It had been a few days since we had seen each other. I detoured to the kitchen, poured Jack a cup of coffee, and picked out a chocolate-frosted doughnut for Jeremy.

I delivered both and sat quietly, reading Abraham Lincoln while Jack did impressions of *both* Phineas and Ferb to Jeremy's continued guffaws. He was having such a good time that he renamed the fish—Phineas being the smaller, bright yellow one.

"Thanks for the coffee," Jack said, sitting after saying good-bye to Jeremy and small-talking with Jeremy's parents. His jet-black hair was an unwashed mess. He did not smell like laundry detergent anymore. "Is everything okay? Your whole family was looking for you. How's Riley?"

"She's good," I replied. *She's coming home. We had a fight. I called her father.* "How are you?"

"Same. You know." He shrugged, taking a sip of coffee.

"Yeah."

"Jeremy is a funny kid," he said.

"You really make him laugh." I kept eye contact, but not as long as Monica, because I felt the beginning of tears in my eyes.

"Same age as Colin," he explained. I watched as his eyes suddenly darted around the room. "Easy peasy." *Where do you go when you're not here? Is your mom okay? Did she go back to work? How do you get here every day?*

"He's lucky to have you."

"Yeah." He held back a hint of a smile.

You can tell me more.

But you don't have to.

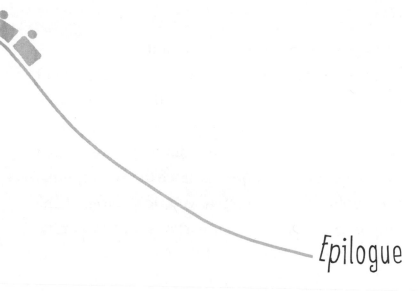

Epilogue

A few days later Riley was home. She used the walker to make it up the brand-new ramp to the front door—quickly, I might add. Archie knew she was coming, too; his face was at the window as we pulled up. When Aunt Maureen helped Riley out of the car, that dog LOST HIS MIND. I thought he was going to break through the window to get to her. Dad knew to go ahead and put him on a leash so he wouldn't knock Riley right off her feet. Not that she would have minded; that girl LOST HER MIND when she saw him, bursting into tears and forgetting for a minute that she didn't quite have her old legs yet. Aunt Elayne held her up when she let go of the walker to wrap her arms around Archie. For a tiny woman, Aunt Elayne is crazy solid.

Elayne had checked out of the hotel and unpacked her suitcase in Grandma's old room. We spent most of the time in the kitchen, or as we called it now, the family room, where we started the day and did most of our talking—and arguing, and apologizing. I promise you, Riley wasn't the only one who used hand gestures and profanity. Although she did come to the table one morning with the UNO wild card taped to her forehead and absolutely nothing nice to say to anybody. Aunt Maureen was not having it.

The ORB kept its place in the middle of the kitchen table and was used so frequently, there was barely any room left in it—turns out everybody had different words and drawings they needed. My favorite one was this:

There was no label. But I know Riley's wolf when I see it, 100 percent.

The End

*(unless you have some words
of your own to add)*

THE
OFFICIAL
RILEY
BOOK

(aka "the ORB")

● I AM

short of breath	in pain	choking	feeling sick	afraid
hungry/thirsty	cold/hot	tired	dizzy	angry

PAIN CHART

LEVEL OF PAIN

10
9
8
7
6
5
4
3
2
1
0

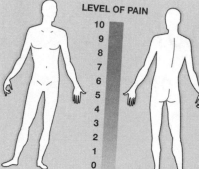

dull	itches
sharp	stings
radiating	hurts/aches
can't move /numb	burns

I WANT PAIN MEDICINE

shot	one pill	two pills

● I WANT

to be suctioned	lip moistened	water / ice	to be comforted	to sleep
tv/video/dvd	call light /remote	quiet	lights off/on	to go home
to sit up	to lie down	to turn left/ right	head of bed up/down	get out of bed

Riley

~~Maureen~~
~~Mom~~
Moo-Moo

~~Uncle Mike~~
Dad

Aunt Paige

Nora

Archie

Aunt Elayne

doughnuts

Harry
Potter

Fries
PAPAS
FRITAS

NY Mets
METS DE
NUEVA YORK

Abe
Lincoln
ABE
LINCOLN

Owl
BÚHO

Summer
VERANO

Tamarin
Monkey
TAMARIN MONO

HORSE / CABALLO

SLIPPER / GATO

Singing

Dancing

Drawing

skateboarding

Taylor
Swift

Jesus

Hell

F-bomb

BATHROOM /
BAÑO

BEDPAN /
ORINAL
DE CAMA

BRAIN

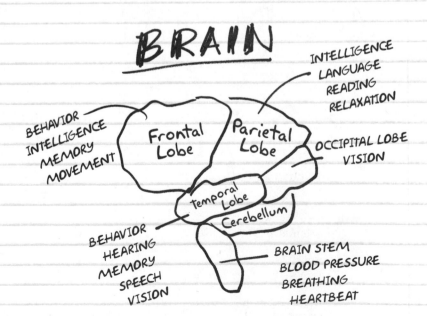

INTELLIGENCE
LANGUAGE
READING
RELAXATION

BEHAVIOR
INTELLIGENCE
MEMORY
MOVEMENT

Frontal Lobe

Parietal Lobe

OCCIPITAL LOBE
VISION

Temporal Lobe

Cerebellum

BEHAVIOR
HEARING
MEMORY
SPEECH
VISION

BRAIN STEM
BLOOD PRESSURE
BREATHING
HEARTBEAT

Visitor's ~~Runner's~~ Log

Name:

DAY	DISTANCE	TYPE (trail, sidewalk, hills, etc)	FEELINGS	COMMENTS
7/1	2m	sidewalk		
7/3	1.5	sidewalk		
7/4	2	Track	Happy fourth!	
7/6	1	park		RAIN!!!
7/8	2.5	Track		with Mari
7/9	1	sidewalk	Excited!	driving to NY Today!
7/11	1	sidewalk		Riley refuses to run! BOO!
today	15min	P.I.C.U.		
yesterday	15min	P.I.C.U.		
??	—	E.R.	—	Beep, Beep.

PATIENT RIGHTS:

A Guide for Patients, Caregivers, and Families

What are your rights? you might ask. Well, they include the right to receive treatment without discrimination as to race, color, religion, sex, national origin, disability, sexual orientation, source of payment, or age.

Riley's TEAM

Bonus drawings
by Sophia

Colin
by Jack

Self-portrait
by Jack

Wolves by Riley

Acknowledgments

I am deeply indebted to my editor, Caitlyn Dlouhy, and to my long-time publisher, Atheneum Books for Young Readers, for supporting this giant leap outside my comfort zone. (And in Caitlyn's case, sometimes really pushing really hard [lovingly] and forcing me even further out!) Thank you to Sophie Hawkes and Grace Meis for their fantastic artwork.

A special thank-you to the NYU Langone Neonatal Intensive Care Unit, where, so many years ago, they held all of our hands; to the NICU nurses who taught us to watch the baby, not the numbers—a lesson that still holds true. And a special thank-you to Katherine Erbe, who had the toughest job of all.

Additional debts are owed to the nurses among my friends, who tirelessly answered my questions and shared their own experiences again and again and again, often leaving me in awe (and in tears).

Finally, to Julia and Abby, who get on all the scary rides with me and hold on tight.